Can a small band of cattle herders defeat a greedy rancher trying to fence in the Open Range?

NOW A MAJOR MOTION PICTURE STARRING . . .

ROBERT DUVALL as Boss Spearman

KEVIN COSTNER as Charley Waite

ANNETTE BENING as Sue

MICHAEL GAMBON as Baxter

ABRAHAM BENRUBI as Mose

DIEGO LUNA as Buttons

DEAN MCDERMOTT as Dr. Barlow

Other *Leisure* books by Lauran Paine:

BORDER TOWN
THE DARK TRAIL
THE RUNNING IRON
TEARS OF THE HEART
LOCKWOOD
THE KILLER GUN
CACHE CAÑON
THE WHITE BIRD
DAKOTA DEATHTRAP

OPEN RANGE

LAURAN PAINE

LEISURE BOOKS  NEW YORK CITY

A LEISURE BOOK®

August 2003

Published by

Dorchester Publishing Co., Inc.
276 Fifth Avenue
New York, NY 10001

Published by arrangement with Hyperion/Touchstone Films. Published by special arrangement with the Golden West Literary Agency.

This book was originally published under the title *The Open Range Men*.

ISBN 0-8439-5261-X

Printed in the United States of America.

OPEN RANGE

Chapter One
A Gray World

Everything had a uniform drabness: the sky, the earth, and everything in between was gray. Sudden downpours from squall winds added to the dreary sameness. Even glimpses of some distant mountains showed them also to be gray.

The old wagon blended into the gloominess. There was a waterproofed texas someone had made by raising a pole underneath the cloth, high in the center so water would run downward instead of accumulating in the center of the top, causing a hazardous sag. There was a shallow shovel-width trench completely around the wagon, which carried off most of the water. The ground beneath the texas was wet but not soggy.

Everything seasoned rangemen could do to mitigate wetness had been done, but after the second day of steady rainfall nothing could keep the moisture out completely. Even the air inside the wagon was damp.

There had been very little warning. One night when the men bedded down they saw a few fleecy clouds in the sky. The clouds looked soiled around the edges but they were not numerous. Sometime during the night the storm had arrived. Its intensity gradually built up from one of those customary summer showers that cattlemen welcomed until it became a genuine gully washer that had not slackened for two days and nights.

The cattle were out there, invisible to the rangemen whenever the cattle were more than a hundred yards away. The same with the horses—two half-ton bay harness animals and eight saddle horses.

This kind of a storm, out in the middle of a thousand miles of rolling-to-flat grassland with a monotonous view in all directions, had an effect on men whose thoughts, habits, and customs had made them individuals who coveted wide open spaces. Suddenly the weather had forced their horizons to shrink way back to the perimeter of the old wagon, along with most of their activities. By the second day of the downpour they had gone from inhabitants of an almost limitless world to being prisoners of an area no more than sixty feet long by about twelve feet wide.

They played poker with a greasy and dog-eared deck of cards. They slept as often as they cared to. They talked about other times, other places, other people and events. Finally, they took to smoking beneath the texas, coat collars turned up, shirts closed all the way to the gullet, hat brims pulled in front and back so water could run off down the sides. The rangemen buckled their chaps into place, leaving the part below the knee swinging free, because leather kept water out, for a while anyway.

The eldest of them was Boss Spearman. Sixty-odd years earlier his mother had named her beautiful little chubby baby boy Bluebonnet because his eyes were the color of the flower, but no one had called him anything but Boss for about half a century.

His mother wouldn't have recognized him now. Boss was a little under six feet tall, lean, scarred, lined, craggy with a shock of rarely combed iron-gray hair. Like all orphaned Texans left on their own in the wake of a ruinous war, Boss Spearman had reached manhood by clawing his way. Whatever was said about him, he was resourceful. He was taciturn among townfolks and strangers, and he was as shrewd as they came, tough and sinewy. His thoughts, movements, and actions were those of a much younger man.

The youngest of the rangemen was a waif called Button, which was a common name for youngsters. Boss and Charley Waite had rescued Button from an alley fight where townsmen in western New Mexico had pitted him against another boy and placed bets on the outcome. Button was getting whipped to a frazzle when Boss and Charley broke it up and took him out to the wagoncamp with them.

Now Button was sixteen, doing a man's work in a man's world, growing like a weed, thin as a rail, with hair the color of dirty straw.

Charley had trailed cattle west with Boss Spearman. He was a little less than average in height, had muscle packed inside a powerful frame, had dark hair and eyes, and could do something few other men ever learned. He could rope equally well with either hand. Charley's full name was Charles Travis Postelwaite. Before he'd reached twenty he shortened it to Charley Waite. He looked to be about forty-five but in fact was thirty-five.

The last of them was well over six feet tall and weighed better than two hundred pounds. He had nondescript dark hair and deep-set gray eyes, a wide mouth, and scars. His name was Mosely Harrison. They called him Mose.

Big Mose, leaning against the tailgate beneath the canvas, was the first to see the rent in the sky far eastward and say, "It's goin' to break up. Look yonder."

But the storm didn't break up. Not for another twenty-four hours, and then it ended the same way it had arrived, silently in the soggy night. When they rolled out in the morning to get a cooking fire started with damp wood, there was only a misty dampness to the air. The downpour had stopped.

For another few days, though, the ground would be too treacherous underfoot to do much, and there were seepage springs everywhere that underlying layers of rock would not allow water to penetrate.

Charley was frying sidemeat. The old pot held the last of their coffee. When the others squatted to eat in silence, Charley rationed out soggy fried spuds, meat, and three baking-powder biscuits to each plate. He sat down with his tin dish. "Nice little rain," he said. "Grass'll be strong all the way into July maybe."

No one else spoke. They chewed, swallowed, and raised more food to their mouths. They washed the food down with the coffee, then put the tin cups and plates aside to roll smokes. The smoking was a ritual. It signified something: the end of a meal, the end of a day, the spiritual or philosophical girding up for something ahead. Maybe a self-reward for having survived a particular event.

Boss tipped ash into the little fire. "My maw used to say don't anything happen it don't bring some good with it." He pointed with his cigarette hand. They'd been having trouble with the wagon's wheels through a month of hot weather. "Them tires and spokes and felloes is as tight as when they was new."

The next morning the sun arrived, huge and orange-yellow with a single cloud in its path toward the meridian. An hour later the ground steamed; the men shed coats and still sweated. They loafed around the wagon doing minor chores until the kid found the horses. One horse anyway. He'd gone out on foot with a bridle draped from one shoulder and a lariat in his right hand.

Boss walked out a ways, remained out there for a while, then returned to lean on the tailgate, scraping mud off his boots as he said, "Not a sight of anything. I got a feeling we're going to set right here for maybe a week before we find all those damned cattle."

Mose Harrison was rubbing mold off a saddle fender. "If the ground was harder, we could take the wagon wherever the cattle are instead of wastin' days finding them and driving them back here."

Boss gazed at the hulking man. "Yeah," he said dryly. "If. All my life it's been, If."

Charley went up front where the wagon tongue was held off the ground by a little wooden horseshoe keg. He sat up there until he saw distant movement, then returned to the tailgate area. "He caught one."

Boss finished cleaning off the mud and pitched the twig into the dying coals of their breakfast fire. "You want to find the other one, Charley?"

When Button finally got back, mud to the knees and leading a roman-nosed, rawboned big sorrel horse with feet the size of dinner plates, Charley went out with an old croaker sack to dry off the animal's back before saddling up.

The heat had been steadily, muggily building up for over two hours. It would have helped if there had been a little air stirring, but the air was stone-still. Visibility, however, was excellent as Charley reined away heading on an angling northwesterly course. Because there were no tracks, finding any animals would be by sight alone.

They would eventually find them. They'd been through worse situations than this many times. Grazing cattle constantly moved, and this sooner or later brought rangemen face to face with just about every inconvenience or obstacle nature or man could devise.

It was simply a matter of finding which way the cattle had drifted, with their heads down and their rumps to the force of the storm.

What made it unlikely that Charley Waite would find the cattle soon was the duration of the storm. The cattle could drift one hell of a distance in two days.

The roman-nosed horse sweated even at a steady walk. Charley did too. So did the ground, but its sweat was a rising faint mist as hot sunlight cooked soggy earth.

There was a lot of territory on all sides. The only barrier was a range of haze-distanced mountains to the north. They seemed to form around the big prairie in a long-spending curve, like a huge horseshoe.

There were no signs of two-legged life, but there were plenty of pronghorns and deer. Charley came up over a landswell and startled a young, tawny yellow cougar eating a rabbit. They looked at each other in surprise for a couple of seconds before the cat broke away with his belly hairs scraping the ground as he fled eastward. Charley could have shot him. He had his saddlegun along. Instead he turned northward along the rise and stood in his stirrups seeking movement. A rising heat haze shortened visibility a little but he could still see for miles.

The land was empty.

He zigzagged over a mile or two looking for tracks. When he found them, finally, he was about ten miles from camp. From this point on he followed cow sign toward those distant mountains. The cattle would not have got that far, but he loped a little anyway. He needed reassurance that they hadn't got up in there, because if they had, it was going to be hard work finding them and driving them back to open country.

The mountains did not seem to be getting any closer no matter how far he rode toward them. What he sought was a sighting or, failing that, the scent of cattle.

What he found was a big calf lying dead. Squawking buzzards surrounded the corpse, too engrossed in feeding to notice his approach until he was close enough to yell and startle them. Most of the birds ran along the ground to get airborne, but several ignored the proximity of the man to tear at the carcass, too hungry to depart immediately.

They finally left when Charley was about a hundred feet from the carcass. He rode closer, sat his saddle studying the dead calf, trying to figure out what had killed it. He gave up on that because the body had been torn and dragged until there was little semblance of its original self. Charley rode northward on the wide, perfectly visible trail of a lot of cattle.

He had not found the brand back there. If he'd cared to dismount and roll the carcass over to expose the right side, he probably could have found it. Boss Spearman, for some private reason, used one C-iron to make three letter Cs on the right rib cage of his cattle. Charley Waite had been with Spearman six years and still did not know what the three Cs stood for.

Some coyotes appeared through stirrup-high grass following the scent of blood. Charley saw them, then lost them, only to see them again in other places. He thought there were about fifteen of the varmints. There was no doubt about what they were seeking and would ultimately find. When that happened the buzzards would leave, and would stay away.

With the sun coming down the far side of heaven to make Charley tip down his hat to protect his eyes, he finally detected dark movement far ahead.

The cattle.

By count there were supposed to be four hundred cows, mostly wet ones with sassy-fat calves, along with about two hundred and fifty big marketable steers and something like fifteen bulls, a bigger ratio than most cattlemen used. But then, most cattlemen had particular ranges; their cows were not always moving.

Charley turned back, satisfied with this part of his mission. Now he concentrated on locating the horses. With them a man could never be as certain of eventual success. True, there had been no lightning and thunder to spook them out of the country, but they could still be a long way off.

Chapter Two
Getting Back to Normal

He found the horses by riding the course of a crooked creek that had the only tree shade for many miles. The horses were absorbing filtered sunshine while simultaneously stamping and flailing their tails at myriads of flying insects.

They were irritable from being bitten and stung, so when Charley came into sight from above them, they did exactly what he had hoped: they stuck their tails in the air like scorpions and ran southward beside the creek until they were tiring, then veered easterly until they were out of creek mud.

He loped in their wake, keeping them in sight. After they'd got their run out, he slackened down to a walk and eased them in the direction of the wagoncamp. It was shading toward dusk when he had the wagon in sight. Small figures up by the wagon tongue would be Boss, Button, and Mose, who had seen the horses coming.

Charley circled wide to reach camp without exciting the horses, who were perfectly willing to rest anyway. He rode in and swung off to peel the outfit from the roman-nosed gelding.

Boss and the kid went to work at the little cooking fire. Mose came over where Charley was upending his outfit to ask if he'd seen any cattle.

They sat on warm, moist earth beneath the canvas to eat while Charley related what he had found. The dead calf was accepted as one of the hazards of the business. Boss said they would head upcountry tomorrow after breakfast and bring the cattle down closer to camp.

He also grumbled because they were out of coffee, saying someone had ought to ride back to that town they'd passed a couple of days earlier for supplies. Button volunteered. The older men acted as though they had not heard him. Boss asked Mose to go, then heaved up to his feet to climb into the wagon in search of his little dented tin lockbox. When he returned he handed Mose several badly worn, greasy green-backs. Then they discussed what would be needed besides coffee, and when it was clear everything could be carried on a saddle horse, they hunted up their bedrolls and settled in for the night.

The moon, which they had been unable to see for the better part of a week, was full and brilliant. Some foraging wolves passed silently during the night, leaving large tracks in the soft ground. A pair of raccoons scouted the camp. Their boldness took them to the grub box, where their scratching awakened Button, the lightest sleeper among the men. He rolled out, pulled on his soggy boots, picked up a stick, and chased the coons away. He stood in the warm, brilliant night for a while, breathing deeply of air that smelled slightly of fermenting vegetation. Then he turned toward his bedroll at about the same time a dog-wolf sat back out yonder somewhere, pointed his muzzle at the moon, and let go with one of the most mournful calls Button had ever heard. It made the hair rise up along the back of his neck.

He dropped the stick and looked slowly in all directions. That wolf had sounded close, but of course he wasn't. Wolves had learned before most animals had that the sour scent of humans meant guns.

"Hey," a voice said from beneath the old wagon. "What're you doing out there?"

Button twisted toward the voice but said nothing. He went back to his blankets, and in the morning no one mentioned having seen him standing there in the moonlight listening to a mournful wolf.

Before sunrise Mose left riding a large seal-brown horse and carrying two croaker sacks rolled and lashed behind his cantle. They figured he would be back tomorrow night; one day to reach the town and make the purchases, and one day getting back. When they had seen the town a week or so earlier, they were driving cattle, which moved much slower than horses.

Charley led the way up where he had seen the cattle. The sun was hot again, so after sighting the critters they hunted creek shade to tank up their horses and to rest for a while.

Boss was in a philosophical mood. Usually when he was like this he lectured Button. Today was no exception. He squinted in the direction of the herd and said, "Boy, when you're on your own, get hired on in some town and learn a trade. Maybe like the mercantile business. Or the cafe business. Even blacksmithing is a good trade. There are lots of trades a feller can learn in a town."

Button was chewing a grass stalk when he said, "I don't like towns. I never liked them."

Boss leaned with his back to a pair of creek willows. "Look at things like they are," he said. "With a trade in a town you always got a roof over your head, a bed up off the ground to sleep in, food no farther away than a cafe, and whether it's hot or cold, you can always stay dry." Boss turned to see what impression his wisdom was having. It seemed to be having very little. Button was leaning on an elbow chewing the length of grass while gazing steadily far out.

Boss glanced at Charley, who simply shrugged and arose to snug up the cinch, remove the hobbles, and rebridle his horse.

They went more than a mile out of their way to get around the cattle, between them and the distant mountains. Boss stood in his stirrups to signal with an upraised arm for them to start down toward the herd.

The cattle were a mixture of slab-sided razorbacks with horns that tipped upward, and red grade animals with white faces, broad backs, and large hams.

Under different circumstances they would have bet that the razorbacks would run at the firstsight of mounted men, but these animals had notbeen without someone on horseback pushing them along since some were calves. They accepted mounted men with something like equal parts of resignation and annoyance.

The herd broke up a little, came together again with a rider on each wing, and finally settled in behind a mottled razorback steer nearly as tall as a saddle horse. He knew what he was supposed to do and where they were going, so he took thc lead and plodded dutifully along.

Button brought up the drag of young calves and their anxious mothers, along with a scattering of lame animals, or just plain lazy ones. Button was always put in the drag. At least this time he needed no handkerchief to keep from being stifled by manure-scented dust.

Today the heat was a little drier, as was the ground. Because there was no hurry, the cattle were permitted to browse as they went along, something else they had become accustomed to.

Two events broke the sameness. The first was a prime young pronghorn who was slow getting out of his bed when the riders came along, perhaps because he thought only the cattle were out there with him.

His mistake. Boss shot him on the run. They had to halt and gut him for carrying. The cows got a mile ahead before the men were ready to ride again.

The second event occurred with the wagon in sight. A short-backed brindle cow who looked as though she was in the last stages of bloat left the drive. All Charley Waite's swearing could not make her go back, so he drew off and watched as she went looking for something she never found: a hiding place amid trees or thick underbrush where she could have privacy while calving.

She didn't have time enough for much of a

search, so she settled for second best, a grassy high landswell that offered an unobstructed view in all directions. She stood skylined up there watching Charley, the nearest potential enemy, scored the ground with her left horn, then with her right, and pawed dirt. She was not challenging the horseman, nor threatening him; she was telling him very plainly to stay away and leave her alone.

He looped his reins and lit up a smoke. When Boss came along Charley said, "It's not coming right. When she passed me, only one foot was out."

They dismounted to wait. The herd went southward with only Button far back to keep it moving.

Deerflies came out of nowhere to pester the waiting men. They kept gloved hands moving; deerflies didn't just bite, they stung.

The cow was up and down several times, lowing and looking back where her straining should have left a calf. Boss lifted his hat to scratch, dropped the hat back down, and smashed his quirley into the ground. Neither man said a word; they had to wait, whether they liked it or not. They could not approach her until she was wringing wet with sweat and too weak from straining to jump and charge them.

Finally, when they saw her beating her head on the ground, they arose, snugged up cinches, mounted, and rode at a walk toward the low topout. When they were about seventy-five feet away, Boss unslung his lariat and rode with it loosely draped around the saddlehorn.

They widened the distance between them so as to approach the panting, wild-eyed cow from far out on both sides. They came together again behind the downed animal. Charley pointed. One jelly-like little hoof was out, along with half a leg. There was no sign of the other hoof.

They rode closer and sat a moment to see if the cow would try to stagger to her feet to charge them. She could not, because she was completely exhausted from straining. When they dismounted, the cow raised her head to try to see them over the enormously distended side of her body, then flung her head down hard against the ground, tongue lolling, eyes bloodshot and glazed.

Charley took the hondo end of Boss's lariat, went up behind the cow, knelt, removed his gloves, and rolled up one sleeve. He probed for the hung-up hoof, found it, got the hoof out where it was supposed to be, looped the rope, and raised his hand.

Boss took one dally on his saddlehorn from the ground, kept the rope in his fist to pay out if he had to, and backed his horse.

Twice Charley signaled for slack; they let the cow pant and groan for a few moments each time, then started up again. The third time the calf came out like the seed being popped out of a grape. Charley freed the rope and flung it away, tailing the calf around in front of the cow, where she could see it and start the cleaning-up process without getting up. Then he quickly mounted his horse and turned away.

But this cow did not have even one charge left in her.

They watched her for a while, then turned to catch up with the drive, Boss coiling his rope as they moved along. He studied the drive up ahead, then looked around the empty countryside, and finally squinted skyward. "No more rain," he said matter-of-factly.

Charley was squinting down where Button was sashaying to keep an old cutback with the herd, and grinned. "Another couple of years, Boss, an' he's going to make a pretty fair hand."

Boss Spearman watched Button until he got the cutback turned into the herd, then looped his rope and said, "It's no life for a kid, Charley. In fact, it's no life for a man. He'd ought to get settled in somewhere. Learn that there's more to life than lookin' at the back end of cows. Maybe in a few years take a wife."

Charley was silent for a while. They loped to catch up and when they hauled back down to a walk he said, "You can't make up somebody else's mind for him. He's living better now than when we found him living out of scrap buckets behind cafes and such."

"Yeah. But this ain't what a young feller had ought to want to do. Charley, we've had trouble ever since we come into this country. Our kind of work is about done for. But even if it wasn't, what do either one of us have to show for it?"

"Well, boss, I got a good saddle, two guns, and my blankets. You got a fortune in cattle. Neither one of us had them things when we was his age."

"That's my point, Charley. We got just about everything we're ever goin' to have in this damned lifetime. But Button, hell, he's ripe for better things."

"Such as?"

"Well, bein' a doctor, or a harness maker. Maybe go to work clerkin' in a big store and someday owning it."

None of those sounded appealing to Charley

Waite, so he put a screwed-up stare on the older man. If they hadn't scuffed over a lot of campfires together, Charley might have held his tongue now. He said, "Too bad you never had a son."

Spearman gazed dead ahead for a long while, then simply said, "Yeah. Maybe."

They picked up the gait, fanned out to bunch up the herd where it was beginning to get too scattered, and kept their wing positions until they were close enough to camp to leave the cattle to themselves.

Button had been picking up twigs as he rode along and had a tidy little bundle when they reached the wagon, where he threw them down before riding over to off-saddle and hobble his horse.

Everyone was mostly silent through supper and afterward, when they eased back to smoke and let their thoughts wander. Boss went off to his blankets, leaving the kid and Charley near the dying fire. Button asked a question out of the blue that caught Waite unprepared. "If a man gets married an' his wife gets heavy an' it's not coming right, what does a man do?"

Charley gained time by leaning with elaborate precision to flip the butt of his quirley squarely into the center of the dying fire. Then he settled back and removed his hat to study the inside of it before answering. "He fetches in a doctor."

"If he's out in a place like this?"

Charley put his hat back on. "A man had ought to know better'n have his woman fifty miles from a town if she's calvy."

Evidently these were not the answers Button had hoped for, so he simply grunted up to his feet and went off in the direction of his bedroll, leaving Charley sitting there stoically for another five minutes, before he rolled up his eyes, wagged his head, and went off to his own bedground.

Chapter Three
A Long Day

They spent most of the following day emptying the wagon and rolling up its waterproofed covering to let hot sunlight reach in and thoroughly dry things.

They also rode for firewood, which could only be found over along the crooked creek. Even that was not very burnable, because creek willows, even bone-dry ones, lacked whatever other woods possessed to burn well.

In the midday heat, they bathed in the creek and dried themselves in the sunlight. They also made a slow ride around the cattle. It was getting past calving season, though with bulls and cows having free choice, calves could come just about any time after February. With old cows they occasionally did not arrive until midsummer or later.

As the sun set, they began watching for Mose.

When he did not appear even after dark they cobbled together a supper of antelope meat with tinned corn and stewed tomatoes.

They ate without comment, their thoughts uncharitable. An hour later, with only moonlight to see by, Boss said, "You don't suppose he got into a poker game, do you?"

Charley had had similar thoughts earlier, had decided Mose' wouldn't do that with someone else's money, and now said so. "Maybe his horse pulled up lame, or maybe he got a late start back."

Nothing more was said about Mose's absence. When Boss eventually arose to seek his blankets, he stood a long time looking southeastward and listening. When he left the area of the dying little fire, he was scowling.

Button, who had been silent up until this time, finally spoke. "He could have got hurt between that town and camp."

Charley nodded. "Maybe. But we'd never find him at night."

Button sat slumped nursing a thin brown-paper smoke, pinching it between his thumb and forefinger. "Charley?"

The older man raised his eyes, turning cautious and wary. The kid sometimes came up with the damndest questions.

"Yeah?"

"Remember that fight Mose got into with those horse ranchers couple months back near that Mex town near the border?"

Waite remembered. Mose hadn't started the fight, the horse ranchers had. When it was over, Mose was bleeding from the nose and had a split lip and raw knuckles. The horse ranchers had four cowboys beaten unconscious and one of the ranch owners, an older, graying man, unable to straighten up. He had gone for his hip holster when Mose had been occupied with two riders, and Mose had somehow managed to kick him squarely between the legs while battering his riders.

"I remember it, kid. I don't expect to ever forget it. That's something about Mose I never could figure out. How can a man be so sort of—well—slow in the head sometimes, and yet be such a smart fighter."

"Maybe he's not back because he got into another fight. Maybe he's lyin' hurt in town or they got him locked up."

Charley gazed at the pale coals that blushed soft red at the slightest breath of moving air. He really had thought Boss should have sent him, or gone himself, rather than send Mose to that town. He said, "Go bed down. Nothing we can do tonight anyway."

Button obediently arose and went toward the front of the wagon where his blankets were. It was the first bedroll he'd ever owned. It wasn't much, three old moth-eaten brown army blankets Boss had dug out and a ground canvas with most of the waterproofing worn off it. But it was his and he treasured it.

Charley had a final smoke for the day and was sitting hunched when Boss appeared soundlessly in his stocking feet, hair awry, solemn as an owl. He sat down like an Indian, neither addressed Charley nor looked at him, but sat there peering into the rusty red ash of their supper fire for a long time before finally speaking.

"I heard the kid," Boss said.

Charley's answer to that was short. "He's worried."

Boss still did not raise his eyes. "You worried?"

Charley trickled bluish smoke while replying. "Yeah, I'm worried. Have been worried since sundown. You should have gone or sent me."

"Mose can look out for himself."

Charley dropped the quirley among the ash. "I know that. But not against a whole town of 'em, Boss."

"This time of year riders pass through towns every blessed day of the week. What's one more stranger?" Boss finally looked across at Charley. "They wouldn't have no idea who he is."

"Then why isn't he sittin' here with us?"

Boss was silent. He was also annoyed. Ever since Charley Waite had been working for him, Charley had shown a very irritating knack for making a statement or asking a question that knocked the props out from under Boss's arguments.

"Well, like Button said, maybe his horse came up lame and he's walking instead of riding."

Charley did not pursue it. Instead he said, "What do you want to do?"

"That's what I came back here to talk about. You'n me could strike out real early to find him. Button can watch the outfit. We'll most likely be back with Mose and the supplies before suppertime."

Charley was agreeable. There was nothing pressing: the cattle were in sight again, the horses weren't too far out, the ground was drying. In another couple of days they'd be able to move the wagon again, then they'd leave this place looking for new grass somewhere else. He nodded and arose. "Meet you here an hour or so before sunup."

They parted and bedded down. The slightly lopsided moon shone eerily silver and the night was quiet right up until its coldest point, an hour or so before daybreak, when Charley heard Boss bringing in two horses.

Charley rolled out, feeling around for his boots, which he upended and shook vigorously to dislodge whatever might have crawled in during the night.

Button called out sleepily from up near the front of the wagon, "Did Mose get back? Is that him back there with the horses?"

Charley was cinching up his belt as he replied. "No, it's Boss. Him and I are goin' back a ways to meet Mose. You go on back to sleep, Button. No need for you to roll out."

When Charley and Boss were saddling their horses, Button came back there rumpled, bootless, and unhappy. "I could go along," he said to Boss. "Three sets of eyes is better'n two sets."

Boss lifted down the stirrup leather after cinching up. He spoke without looking around. "No need. We'll find him. Someone had ought to stay with the wagon, Button."

"No one's going to bother it, Boss. We haven't seen a single person out here since we set up camp."

Boss turned, reins in hand, ready to mount. "We won't be gone long. I always feel better about leavin' the wagon if someone is close around." He watched Charley swing up and made a parting remark to the youth. "You been working hard lately anyway, Button. You deserve a little loafing time. Maybe later if you want to you could ride out and look for calvy cows that're in trouble so's when we get back we can take care of 'em."

Though they did not look back, neither of them felt exactly comfortable. Boss was buttoning his old coat under his neck when he said, "One of these days we got to take him into a town and get him a haircut, maybe some new pants, a decent shirt, and a cafe-cooked meal."

Charley said nothing.

It was cold, which it always was before dawn, even in central New Mexico. And if they held to their present course with the cattle of north-by-northwest, they would eventually get up into higher country where, regardless of how hot the days were, the nights were never warm.

Charley had half expected to find Mose in camp this morning. Maybe it was more a hope than an expectation. Now, with the first hint of sunrise along the horizon, he was genuinely worried.

But he leashed his imagination and thought only of something innocuous like a lame horse or maybe Mose's bedding down and oversleeping after visiting a town.

They aimed in the direction instinct told them would be the proper course and held to it until sunrise. Then they quartered, each man making an individual wide sashay until Boss found what they sought and stood in his stirrups to wave with his hat.

Charley approached at a lope. Boss pointed to the single set of shod-horse tracks with one hand while reaching with the other to unbutton the topmost part of his coat.

They chewed jerky as they followed the tracks.

With the sun climbing, Charley veered off to look for a second set of tracks. They would mean that Mose had passed them in the darkness on his way to the wagoncamp.

He did not find another set. In fact, he did not find any horse sign at all, shod or unshod. He saw pronghorn tracks, which looked a lot like goat tracks, and he found a soft place in a swale where wolves had left their marks while moving straight northward. If a wolf had a lick of sense he'd never let daylight catch him out in open country.

They halted at noon to let the horses crop grass while they hunkered and smoked. Boss had been getting less communicative for the last couple of hours. He did not speak now when he held out a sputtering sulfur match to light their smokes.

Charley said, "If we pick up the gait this afternoon, by late evenin' we'd ought to be able to see rooftops."

Boss smoked, squinted into the distance, and said nothing. Later, when they were mounting, Boss finally spoke. "If he never got clear of that town, Charley, it'd be a safe bet he ran into trouble."

Charley Waite knew exactly what kind of trouble his companion was thinking about. "Let's wait until we've covered another few miles before makin' guesses."

They loped, walked for a mile or two, then loped again. There was no danger of losing the tracks. If it hadn't rained a week earlier they would have to ride more slowly now to hunt for sign. Something, anyway, was in their favor.

If they'd had an idea they would have to ride the full distance to that town when they'd left the wagon, they would have covered more ground earlier.

With afternoon advancing they made an effort to correct that mistake. But they still did not see rooftops before dusk, even though they could tell by the faint smoke scent coming out to them from kitchen stoves that they were not very far out.

Finally they could see lamplight. This was irregular at first, coming from scattered homes. Closer, they saw a solid rank of lights where the town's main roadway lay.

They had no idea what the place was called until they rode up onto a washboardy roadbed and turned southeasterly in the direction of those lights and encountered a faded old sign that said *Harmonville.* The sign at one time had also given the population, but a shotgun blast had since obliterated that piece of the sign.

They rode down the middle of Main Street, the only movement the full length of the road. There was activity at a saloon on the east side of the road, and nearly opposite but a few doors southward there was more activity where someone had established a cardroom and poolhall.

Nearly all the stores were locked up for the night, windows dark and steel shutters in place. Three horses dozed in front of the jailhouse. Light shone from two narrow, barred windows.

They rode down to the livery barn, piled off, handed over their reins, and when the nightman, old, thin as a snake, with milky whiteness to his eyes, asked if they figured to stay in town all night, Boss's reply was curt. "No longer'n it takes for us to find what we come for, friend."

The old man, almost ghostly beneath a hanging coal-oil lantern with a sooted glass mantle, had another question. "Maybe I can help, gents. Who is it you're lookin' for? I know everyone in town and for miles beyond, because I been here since Harmonville was called Fort Harmon an' there was soldiers to chase off the consarned In'ians."

Boss and Charley studied the old man. He seemed to want to be genuinely helpful. He also seemed so frail that a light wind would carry him away. Boss said, "A big feller. Real big, needin' a haircut, about twenty-five."

The old man gazed steadily at Boss for a long time without parting his lips. He looked them both up and down. "Yeah, I know who you're talkin' about. Looked like he'd been livin' out of his saddlebags most of his life. Got some scars on his face."

"You know where we can find him?" Charley asked.

The old man knew. "Up yonder in the jailhouse."

"What'd he do to get in there?"

"I wasn't there so I can't say exactly what happened, but the story is that some range cattlemen started in on him at the general store, and he hurt three of 'em before Marshal Poole come up in back and hit him over the head with his gunbarrel."

The old man paused, his milky gaze sliding from Spearman to Waite. "Doc Barlow patched him up . . . Does he ride with you gents?"

Boss nodded his head.

The old man said, "Mister, I can tell you one thing maybe you'd ought to know. Folks in the Fort Harmon country hate freegrazers worse'n they used to hate In'ians. You might want to bear that in mind when you're talking to the town marshal."

Chapter Four
The First Warning

By the time they got up to the jailhouse, only one of the tethered horses was still dozing at the tie-rack out front. When they entered, a long-legged, lean man with sandy hair and testy eyes turned from filling two cups with coffee at the woodstove to stare at them. He had a five-pointed star on his vest.

The other man was heavyset and slouching in a chair as though he'd been relaxing there for some time. He was older than the town marshal, in his late fifties or early sixties. His face was round, ruddy, and beard-stubbled. He showed no expression as he stared at Boss and Charley. Neither did the lawman until Boss said, "Evening, gents. My name's Spearman. This here is Charley Waite."

Neither man spoke. The marshal turned back to filling the cups, handed one to the heavyset man, and took the other one over to a desk chair with him. He said, "I'm Al Poole, town marshal. This is Denton Baxter. He ranches north of town near the foothills. What can I do for you?"

Marshal Poole did not ask his visitors to be seated. Charley Waite got the impression that both Poole and Baxter not only knew who he and Boss were, but had not been surprised when they had walked into the jailhouse office.

Evidently, Boss had the same feeling, or else he sensed hostility, because he remained standing, thumbs hooked into his shell belt, as he spoke bluntly. "Down at the livery barn they told us you have a friend of ours in your cells. His name is Mose Harrison."

Denton Baxter's eyes never left Boss; his face remained expressionless. Marshal Poole put his coffee cup aside when he spoke. "Yeah. I got him here. He started a fight in the general store."

Boss wagged his head. "Mose don't start fights. He just finishes 'em."

Poole looked hard at Spearman. "I said he started it and you said he didn't. That sounds maybe like you're calling me a liar."

Charley could see Boss's shoulders straightening, and he spoke before Boss could. "Is he hurt, marshal?"

Poole's gaze drifted to Charley. "He got hit over the head. I had the town doctor patch him up. Right now he's sleeping. When he wakes up he'll have a headache. Otherwise he seemed all right to me."

Boss's face was reddening as he stared downward at the seated lawman. He knew exactly what was behind this; he'd had this and other forms of harassment since he'd entered New Mexico from

Texas. But he did not mention what he knew. Instead he said, "You got a charge against him, marshal?"

Poole deliberately sipped coffee before replying. "Yeah. Incitin' to fight. Disturbin' the peace. You want him back, Mister Spearman?"

"Yes."

For the first time both the seated men showed something in their faces, the hint of a cold smile. Al Poole nodded very slowly without taking his eyes off Boss. "All right. You pay the fines an' you can have him. Hundred dollars for fightin'. Hundred dollars for disturbin' the peace. How's that sound to you?"

Boss's answer was sharp. "Like highway robbery." His voice had a deadly soft tone.

Charley braced. Marshal Poole's eyes didn't change, but his wide mouth drew out flat as he leaned to arise. The older man spoke for the first time, ignoring Poole's obvious quick-rising temper. He did not raise his voice as he said, "It's a lot of money, ain't it? Maybe we can figure something out. There's always two sides to everything." He waved a thick, work-callused hand in the direction of the stove. "Have a cup of coffee, Mister Spearman."

Boss did not move.

Baxter put the hand back in his lap. "Your man's horse is down at the public corrals. His rig's at the livery barn. You can take him with you when you leave town tonight. An' first thing in the morning you hitch up your wagon, get your damned freegrazing cattle moving, and keep 'em moving until you're out of the Fort Harmon country."

Seconds passed as Boss stared at the slouching

older man. He had known what was behind all this the moment that scarecrow down at the livery barn told him what happened to Mose. Established cowmen, and most townsmen as well, were hostile to the kind of cattlemen Boss Spearman represented, because their cattle grazed through a country and kept going, leaving behind for local ranchers eaten-off grass. What the livery barn nightman said had been becoming increasingly prevalent over the years: freegrazers were no longer predominant, as other stockmen had taken up land, settled in, and—whether they had legal right or not—staked claims to vast grazing areas that they had used to build up extensive ranches.

What Boss had said to Charley only a day or two earlier during their discussion of Button's future had been based on his knowledge that the free-graze method of drifting cattle over open range, owning no land, simply using it, was becoming increasingly unpopular among livestock men. There had been out-and-out battles between established cowmen and freegrazers. Both Boss and Charley had been through a few of those confrontations.

Boss stood gazing at the slouching, heavyset man, who met his stare without blinking. Obviously, Denton Baxter, who appeared to own Town Marshal Poole, was not just a power in the Fort Harmon country, but was also one of those ranchers whose opposition to freegrazers was deep and unalterable.

As the two older men confronted each other in silence, Marshal Poole made a drawling comment to Spearman. "Times change. Most folks manage to change with them. A few holdouts never do.

Mister Spearman, we knew when you grazed into our territory, an' we know what you been doing since you set up your wagoncamp out yonder. What we been waiting for is to see you strike camp and move on. You haven't done it."

Denton Baxter quietly said, "He will, marshal. Mister Spearman looks like a reasonable man to me. Why don't you go see if his rider's able to ride? If he is, fetch him up here so these gents can get back to their camp."

After the lanky, rawboned marshal had taken his key ring and gone down into the cellroom, Denton Baxter shifted in his chair, showed a smile, and said, "Have some coffee, gents. It'll be a long ride back in the cold."

When he finished speaking, Denton heaved up out of his chair and went to the stove to refill his own cup. He turned around and stood wide-legged, no longer smiling, tawny eyes fixed on Boss Spearman. "Three years ago a freegraze outfit come into the country up along the foothills where I own land and run cattle. Something happened one night. Their cattle got stampeded all over the countryside, their wagon caught fire while they was out tryin' to find their cattle, an' when one of them boys was ridin' a rim he got shot off his horse in the dusk." Baxter drank half his coffee before continuing. "Three days later they was gone with what cattle they'd found."

Baxter went back to his chair and sat down holding his half-empty cup. When Marshal Poole came up out of the cellroom herding a puffy-faced, bruised, and shuffling Mose Harrison, Baxter went to the marshal's desk, produced a bottle of whiskey, poured a cup, and handed it to Mose.

Boss and Charley were shocked at Mose's appearance. He hadn't just been hit over the head but kicked and beaten too. He took the whiskey to a bench and sat down as he forced an ill smile at Boss and Charley. He drank, blew out a fiery breath, and finally spoke. "Glad to see you. I'd like to get back to camp."

Boss Spearman turned a cold look at Marshal Poole. "Looks like someone put the boots to him after he was down."

Poole said, "Does it?" He tossed a worn old shell belt and holstered Colt atop the desk. "Take 'em with you, Mister Spearman. You'll be too busy getting under way to come back to Harmonville, I expect, and that'll be just fine. There won't be no more trouble."

They left the office with Mose between them, walking in the direction of the livery barn. Mose said nothing. He had a large bandage beneath his old hat, his gaze was dull, and his attitude was indifferent. They got him astride under the solemn gaze of that milky-eyed old nighthawk and adjusted the croaker sacks full of provision. He rode up through Harmonville between Boss and Charley. Two men leaning out front of the jailhouse watched him depart from town with his friends, then they strolled in the direction of the town saloon.

The night was cold, but moonlight made visibility better than it had been when Spearman and Waite had first left the wagoncamp.

Mose did not say ten words the full distance back, and until the effects of the whiskey wore off an hour or so after sunrise, he seemed almost normal.

An hour or so before they had camp in sight,

he started to sag in the saddle. With his condition deteriorating from that point on, Boss and Charley had to support him on his horse.

Button was nowhere around when they reached the wagon. They helped Mose down and guided him to canvas shade behind the wagon, where they settled him on his blankets, removed his hat and boots, and went back to care for the horses. Charley said, "I wonder how many of those bastards it took to do that."

Boss's stone-set lips did not part. He methodically hobbled the horse, removed his outfit, waited until Charley was ready, then led the way back to the wagon, with saddle, bridle, and blanket over one shoulder.

Mose was sleeping soundly.

They upended their outfits in the shade and emptied the croaker sacks, made a little fire to cook by, and were finishing their coffee when Button returned in a loose lope. He had seen the rising smoke of their fire. When he strode toward the wagon and saw Mose's bandaged head, discolored, swollen, sweaty face, he stopped in his tracks. Charley got him untracked.

"Have some coffee, made fresh for a change. Where you been?"

Button came up and sat on the ground, still staring at Mose. "What happened to him?"

Charley waited for Boss to reply. "He run into a little trouble in that town."

"Looks like more'n a little trouble," Button said, filling a cup with coffee. After a while he asked Boss a question that indicated he had sorted through possibilities to arrive at the correct one. "Are we goin' to move on?"

Spearman tossed wet grounds into the little fire

before replying. "We always do, don't we, once we've grazed off a place?"

Charley watched Boss get to his feet and walk over to where Mose was sleeping, his back to the fire. Button started to speak, but Charley held up a silencing hand until Boss walked up toward the front of the wagon to roll a smoke and lean in thought. Then Charley said, "Don't ask questions. Just leave things be for a while."

Button looked into his coffee cup. "There was three riders scoutin' up the herd this morning. I didn't see 'em arrive. I was siftin' through lookin' for hung-up calvy cows when I noticed some of the critters starin' out there. And there they was, sitting maybe a half mile out. Just sittin' out there looking at the cattle. We're in for it again, aren't we?"

Charley dumped grounds from his tin cup and tossed the cup toward the grub box. It landed inside and rattled other tin utensils. The sharp noise made Mose groan and flinch in his sleep.

Charley Waite, who was a thoughtful man, rarely hasty about anything including judgments or decisions, answered Button slowly while gazing at their badly beaten friend. "Yeah, we're in for it again, unless we head out within the next day or two." Charley watched the gangling youth's expression grow troubled. He made a poor effort to be cheerful. "About time to move on anyway, isn't it?"

Button's gaze came up slowly. "How many did it take? Charley, they don't own this land, do they? Well then, what right they got to beat a man like that because he rides with an outfit that's got as much right to graze over it?"

Mose was awake and thirsty. Charley got a canteen and knelt to hold it for him, but Mose's strength was returning; he held the canteen without assistance and drank deeply, handed the canteen back, and raised a swollen hand to gingerly explore the bandage and ask who had put it up there.

"Some doctor down in Harmonville," Charley replied. "Looks like a real professional job, Mose."

Mose saw Button staring, and smiled. "It's nothing. Hell, I been hurt worse than this and didn't even stop talking. Button, how'd things go out here?"

"Pretty much like always. Damned horses drifted like they usually do. Mose, you look—"

"Like you're picking up," Charley said, cutting in swiftly. "How about something to eat?"

Mose pushed up into a sitting position and winced. His entire body ached. Charley pretended not to notice as he said, "Button, stir up the fire. Swab out the fry pan."

Boss walked back where he'd heard their voices and gazed a long time at Mose. Then he went rummaging for a bottle of Taos Lightning, which he poured into a tin cup for the injured big man. He, too, forced an appearance of normalcy, but the look in his eyes was as cold and hard as granite.

While they ate he said even less than usual. Charley, who understood Boss Spearman best, heaved an inner sigh. He had seen Boss with his back to a wall before: That expression meant he was not going to strike camp meekly and start the herd moving again, as the town marshal and that possum-bellied cowman with the false smile had told him to do.

The day was wearing along. For a change, it was

neither muggy nor particularly hot. The sky was flawless. Because of that rainstorm followed by several hot days, grass was growing faster than cattle could eat it off. The land was empty as far as a man could see, giving the natural splendor a deceptive appearance of tranquility.

Chapter Five
The Next Day

The following morning Boss said nothing about moving on. After breakfast they left Mose resting in camp and rode out among the cattle. Button had not found any hung-up calvy cows the previous day, but the men sifted through the herd today anyway, leaving Charley to suspect that Boss's mind was not on what he was doing. Every now and then he would straighten up in the saddle and gaze far out and around as though seeking something. Charley knew what he was looking for, and also watched, but there were no horsemen out there.

Button found a sweating razorback cow with her head lower on one side. She was wringing wet with sweat, and rolled bloodshot eyes as Button passed by. He halted at a discreet distance and watched her for a while, then hunted up the older men.

They rode back with him. The cow was slobbering and tossing her head. Boss sighed. "Broke the tip off her damned horn." Charley nodded; he knew as well as Boss did what the razorback's trouble was. He also knew that this time it was going to make pulling a calf look like a Sunday picnic.

They sent Button back to the wagon for the medicine box. During his absence, Boss alternately watched the slobbering cow and raked the countryside for sign of horsemen. There were none in sight but the cow was acting crazier by the moment.

When Button loped back, Boss told him to go out a ways with the medicine box and stay out of the way. Then he and Charley took down their ropes, shook out loops, and walked their horses straight at the cow. She would have fought them if they got too close, even if she didn't have trouble enough to make her wild. She stopped shaking her head, lowered it, pawed dirt, bawled, slobbered, and charged. Boss halted with his loop on the right side. He allowed the cow to get within a hundred feet of him before reining to the left. The cow was coming too fast to change direction at that distance even though she tried by corkscrewing her body and slamming both front hooves sideways.

Boss went closer, rolled his loop twice, and cast it. Charley was already coming in from the opposite side so that when Boss picked up his slack in fast dallies and rode away dragging the fighting cow, she bawled, flung slobbers, and jammed both front legs into the ground, resisting the pulling as Charley got behind her to one side. He made a low cast, caught both hind legs at the pasterns, took fast dallies, and set his horse up to brace against the shock when the cow came to the end of the rope.

She teetered, still fighting wildly, until she could no longer maintain balance, then fell on her left side, pawing with her front legs, trying to gather herself to jump up, which she could not do as long as they had her stretched out.

Boss bellowed for Button and was just dismounting as the youth rode up. Boss gave a little slack and switched his dallies from his own saddlehorn to Button's as he took the medicine box and said, "Keep the slack out, boy. Back your horse if she gets any slack but don't choke the old fool to death."

Button's face was chalk white as he took the tag end of Boss's lariat. There was no prior training for most of the emergencies cattlemen encountered. Button could rope passably well, but this was different. He'd seen them spread-eagle cattle before, but watching was different from doing. He was concentrating so hard on keeping the cow strung out that he didn't hear Charley until he'd yelled twice. "Don't choke her! Give a little slack!"

Boss got up to the cow from behind her, away from those flailing front feet, and dropped to one knee as though he did this every day and there were no danger. He pulled out a pocketknife, pinned the cow's head with his weight, and whittled at the broken tip of her horn until he had trimmed the ragged hole and had enlarged it slightly, then he turned to open the box and rummage until he found a thick blue bottle. He uncorked it with his teeth, stifled a cough as fumes went up his nose, waited until Charley had taken up more slack, then leaned with sweat running down his face, forcing the cow's head still for several seconds and pouring some of the contents of the blue bottle into the holed horn.

The cow was making strangling sounds. She was fighting so hard for breath that she was probably not even conscious of the big older man working on her. Even after he poured fluid into her horn she did not heed him.

Boss methodically stoppered the bottle and placed it back in the wooden box. He stood up to mop off sweat and looked over at Button. The kid's jaw muscles were bulged, his eyes fixed on the cow. Then Boss knelt and yelled to the youth.

"Lots of slack, son, fast! Jump your horse ahead!"

Button obeyed. Boss dropped atop the cow's head, fumbling for the lariat. The moment he yanked it slack the cow sucked down a huge lungful of air; so much oxygen at once nearly overwhelmed her. This was the brief instant Boss needed to wrench the loop loose and fling it aside.

Charley backed his horse as the cow got both front feet beneath her, ready to spring up and charge as Boss ran toward his horse. Charley yanked her back down from behind each time she bawled in fury and tried to spring to her feet. He did not ride up enough so she could kick frantically free of his heeling rope until Boss was in the saddle with the medicine box.

Boss took the slack rope from Button and said, "Run for it!"

Button and Boss raced away with the gasping, wild-eyed razorback cow glaring after them. Charley was coiling his rope as he stood in his stirrups while his mount trotted clear.

From a decent distance all three of them stopped, turned, and watched as the cow braced her front legs wide and began to furiously shake her head. Boss sighed, cleared his throat, spat aside, and said, "You did right well, Button. What a man's got to watch for is that he don't get excited and choke 'em to death."

Button was sweating even under his shirt, and his hands were shaking, so he gripped the saddlehorn with them. "What was wrong with her?"

"Any time a critter busts a horn during fly time of year, they get maggots in the core of the horn. Someday when you do the doctoring you'll hear the flies in there buzzing. It drives a cow crazy. If you don't get rid of the flies and the maggots she'll really be crazy and never get over it. Crazier'n a pet 'coon."

"What did you do?"

"Poured chloroform into the horn. See how she's shaking her head? If we dared, we could ride up to her right now an' you'd see the dead flies an' maggots being flung out of the little hole. They come out in globs. We better ride on."

Button used a sleeve to push off sweat. As the horses began moving he twisted to watch the razorback cow. She was still rattling her horns but was no longer acting crazy.

By the time they reached Charley, he had tied his lariat into place and was sitting calmly, hands atop the saddlehorn, looking toward the northwest, up where those distant mountains appeared clear as glass.

He said, "Four this time, Boss."

He was correct. Instead of three horsemen sitting beyond gunshot range watching them as Button had seen them the day before, this time there were four riders.

Boss spat and dryly said, "The country's filling up."

Charley was thinking of something else: something that bulky old cowman had said in the jailhouse office about cattle being stampeded. That was in his mind because of what else they'd said down in Harmonville: The freegrazers were supposed to have struck camp and started moving the cattle today, this morning in fact.

Four armed men could start a stampede very easily with guns and shouts and racing horses. Charley rolled and lit a smoke. "You want to load up and move out, Boss?"

Spearman had no answer. It would have been reasonable to say yes or no, but he said nothing. He sat easy, watching the distant horsemen from beneath the tipped-down brim of his old hat, silent for a very long time.

Finally he said, "Charley, which way you reckon they'll go when they leave?"

Waite offered a simple answer. "Let's find out." He squeezed his horse and started riding slowly in the direction of the watchers. Boss and Button rode on either side of him. They covered several hundred yards before the watchers turned without haste to head back the way they had come, toward the distant foothills but on an easterly slant.

Boss said, "All right. That's good enough. Let's go back to camp."

None of this made any sense to Button, but he had been learning prudence lately so he loped along without asking a single question.

When they got back, Mose had done something

that surprised them. He had gone over to that willow creek, taken an all-over bath, had walked back, and was coaxing a little cooking fire to life wearing his boots and britches but no shirt.

He had bruises in front and in back, which he ignored as the others came up into canvas shade and sank down. He grinned at them from a battered face topped by a turbanlike bandage that was not as white as it had been the day before.

"Spuds, salt beef, and biscuits. How's that sound?"

It sounded wonderful. More so because big Mose seemed almost completely recovered from his beating, although the marks of it were glaringly obvious and probably would remain so for a week or two.

The mood was light as they sat close with their tin plates and cups. Boss did not say very much, but he teased Button as he usually did when his mind was not occupied with problems. Charley, though, watched Boss and speculated. Boss had something on his mind.

Mose finally told them about the fight in the general store. It had started when three rangemen had strolled in as he was going over his list of supplies with the storekeeper. They had stood on both sides of Mose at the long counter, listening to the talk as Mose and the storekeeper went down the list to tally up the expense. One of them taunted him by saying, "By golly, ain't that downright remarkable? It can read."

Another cowboy said, "Naw, that ain't so much, Slim. Once I seen a man who had a bear about as dirty an' shaggy as this feller who could count with his paws."

Mose said the storekeeper had suddenly turned

to depart, leaving Mose counting up the money for the supplies. The third cowboy, Mose told them, was a tall man with a tied-down ivory-handled six-gun and a long pockmarked face. He walked slowly over, tapped Mose on the back, and when Mose turned, the tall man swung.

"I knew it was coming," Mose told them. "I caught his wrist in the air and fetched it down hard across my upraised leg. The bone snapped like a twig. The other two come at me swingin' like windmills. I got hit a few times, nothing much. I got one by the throat and flung him into the iron stove. The last one, he was stoppin' his charge. Maybe he would have run. But I jumped first, got most of his shirt in my left hand, and hit him three, four times in the face until he was limp as a rag. . . . That's all I recollect until I come around over in the jailhouse hurt all over. Someone hit me from behind. I guess everyone put the boots to me after that. At least that's what the doctor told me. He was friendly and all."

Boss got the whiskey bottle and poured a little into each coffee cup. He poured little more than a spoonful into Button's cup. Even though he'd done a man's work today and had done it well, he was still a button.

They loafed away the evening, replete and relaxed. Charley still watched Boss. Mose was the first to leave the fire. Button was next. Charley made the coals hiss by pouring coffee dregs atop them.

He put the cup aside and was methodically rolling a smoke when he said, "What's on your mind?"

Boss had dumped his hat aside. From the bridge of his nose to the hairline, his skin was as white as snow. Below the bridge of his nose it was weathered a uniform shade of bronze tinted with a faint redness.

He scratched his head without looking at Charley. "I hate to owe someone something and not pay 'em," he said, looking briefly sideways at Charley Waite before returning his gaze to the sizzling coals.

Charley lit up, trickled smoke upward, and faced the older man. "Yeah. Well . . . ?"

"They'll return from the same direction, Charley."

Charley nodded. "Yeah." He inhaled and exhaled slowly. "Boss, it'll stir up a hornet's nest."

"Maybe. What do you expect we should do, tuck our tails and run like they told us to do?"

Charley continued to smoke over an interval of silence before answering. One thing he'd learned in his lifetime was that there were times to lash out and times not to. Right now, with not just the lawman against them but probably every damned rancher and range rider in the territory, and only the Lord knew how many that meant, was not a time to lash out. But Charley also knew he'd be wasting his breath trying to make these points with Boss Spearman, so he said, "We're goin' to get stampeded if we don't, and we're goin' to get ourselves into a damned war if we do."

Boss spoke crisply. "Exactly. For a damned fact. Now then, suppose the pair of us go out there and catch them before they start their run on the herd?"

Charley squinted into the gloom. "Baxter struck me as a mean feller, Boss. He also struck me as a man who owns the law around here, and if that's so, why then he's most likely got a hell of a lot of influence everywhere else."

Boss peered at Charley through the shadows. "What the hell are you goin' to do, Charley? Sit here in camp while I go up there and break it up before it gets started?"

Charley dropped his smoke into the cooling coals and stood up. "I guess not. . . . Sometimes I wished I'd listened to my grandmaw. She wanted me to apprentice out to a printer back in Sioux Falls. She said the printed word was the most important thing in life, next to religion."

Boss chuckled at his companion as they went after their horses.

Chapter Six
A Night to Remember

The moon was a long time arriving. For their purpose, weak light from a limitless expanse of bluish-white stars made it possible for them to cover a couple of miles with visibility foreshortened to the area immediately ahead.

The night was still warm, but they wore coats because before they returned to the wagon the night would have turned cold.

They halted a couple of times to listen, which Charley thought was not really necessary, but when Boss Spearman was doing something like this he was as wary as an Indian. Which was probably a good way to be, under the circumstances.

Excluding that dog-leg creek west of the wagon with its willows, there were few pilot points even during daylight. At night men had to ride by the seat of their pants.

Both Boss and Charley were good at it; where

they eventually halted, both men were satisfied there would have been shod-horse marks on the ground if it had been light enough to make them out. This was where those four watchers had been.

They swung to the ground, testing the night. There was not a sound. Boss hunkered in front of his horse peering eastward. "Be fine with me if they didn't come," he said quietly, and although Charley agreed, he did not say so.

A ground owl came out of his hole thirty or forty feet distant, made a startled squeak because he had picked up the scent even before he saw the four big lumpy shapes, sprang into the air, and made whispery sounds as he frantically beat his wings to get away.

Boss settled on the ground still facing eastward and listening for sound from that direction as he said, "I hope old possum belly is with them. He sat in that jailhouse office sort of sneering and letting his lawman lay down the law until he figured it was time to show us that he an' not the lawman gave the orders around here."

Charley, who had also taken a strong dislike to Denton Baxter, had something to add. "He won't be, Boss. His kind don't do things themselves, they hire other men to do things for them. But I got a hunch we'll meet again—Baxter and us."

Boss was silent for a long time. Silent and motionless, until he slowly raised a gloved hand. Charley heard nothing. He even got belly-down with an ear to the ground, but picked up nothing. Boss turned and winterly smiled. "Well, well, they're coming."

Now, finally, Charley heard the faint sounds of riders with rein chains, spur rowels, and dry leather. He did not hear hooffalls until he heard a gravelly voice say, "Like last time, the old man'll gather up a lot of lost cattle after them bastards is run out of the country."

Someone else laughed. "If that happens often enough he'll make more money gathering stampeded critters than he'll make trailing down to rail's end each autumn and peddlin' off the beef."

A voice with a higher pitch to it offered a precaution. "It won't be so funny if that big one catches us. My back's still sore as a boil where he flung me into that stove."

That remark brought up a fresh topic among the oncoming but as yet invisible horsemen. Gravel-voice said, "Too bad that was Butler's right arm he busted over his leg. A gunfighter ain't no good with a busted gun arm. . . . But when it heals and he's ready, Butler'll square things up. He told me at the doctor's place he was goin' to find that big man and shoot him from the knees up, a little at a time."

Charley leaned to brush Boss's arm. He could vaguely make them out. Both Charley and Boss unwound up off the ground, turning for their booted Winchesters. They stood like statues, carbines in the crook of their arms, one hand raised to clamp down hard if either of their horses offered to greet the strange horses, and watched as the four riders passed directly in front of them traveling due west.

They knew where the herd was or they wouldn't have been riding in that direction. Boss turned and nodded to Charley. Both men knelt to hobble their animals, after which they struck out on foot to keep abreast of the northward riders, giving ground a little until they could not see the horsemen, to be sure that the horsemen could not see them either, then they paralleled the strangers by sound.

The moon was coming. For a while it was little more than half a silver cartwheel above the farthest rims and peaks, but its light increased visibility a little. It was no longer full. Even so, Boss and Charley had to drop farther southward to avoid being seen.

When gravel-voice said, "Hell, we're wastin' time," Boss began to move closer. He was up where he could see the riders with Charley to the east a few yards when he made a spurt to get slightly ahead of the unsuspecting horsemen.

The horsemen were riding relaxed and unwary, right up to the moment that Boss shouldered his Winchester, cocked it, and called out.

"That's far enough! Don't take another step!"

The horses hauled to a dead stop without their riders' lifting a rein hand. The horses were quicker at perceiving danger than the men had been.

Charley came up from their left side, knelt, and also cocked his carbine. The sound of oiled steel sliding over oiled steel on their left completed the surprise. From his position, Charley could see them clearly outlined in the increasing moonlight.

Boss gave an order. "Get down. Step to the head of your horses. One bad move and you're going to hell."

They dismounted, moved up, and stood like stones, silent and motionless. Charley stood up, eased the dog down on his Winchester, and approached them from the left. They could see him clearly, but except for glancing around when he walked up, they were more concerned about the one they could see only vaguely who was up ahead aiming his weapon at them.

Charley grounded his Winchester, freed his coat for access to his holstered Colt, and said, "Shuck your weapons." He neither raised his voice nor sounded particularly menacing, but the horsemen obeyed him. They were recovering from shock, but slowly. Their astonishment had been complete.

Charley went up where he could see their faces. One of them seemed to recognize him because he made a little gasping sound.

Boss came forward from in front, Winchester held low in both hands. He and Charley returned the looks they were getting throughout a moment of silence.

Boss said, "Which one of you's got a sore back?"

No one answered.

Charley swept his right hand back and downward as Boss headed for the riders, stopped three feet from the foremost man, whose coat was unbuttoned and whose holster was empty. He pushed the Winchester muzzle into the man's soft parts. "Which one?" he asked again.

The man jerked his head. "Gus."

Boss pushed the speaker away with this gun muzzle and turned upon the man nearest to him to the right. "You're Gus?"

He didn't get an answer, just a nod of the head.

Boss eased down the carbine's hammer and swung the weapon like a club. The blow sounded like someone striking a sack of grain. Gus went over sidways and scrabbled against the ground with both hands until Boss stepped beside him, placed the carbine muzzle against his back, and cocked it. Gus wilted to the ground and did not move except to breathe in little grunts. He was injured but, worse, he was very frightened. He said, "Wait a minute, mister."

Boss did not move the gun away.

Gus risked a twisted look upward. Boss's granite expression must have convinced him he was one breath away from shaking hands with *Señor Satán*, because he blurted words out, running them all together.

"Wait a minute, it wasn't my idea to jump that feller in town. That's who you're mad about, ain't it mister? It wasn't my idea at all it was Mister Baxter sent us to call him an' rough him up because we knew he was one of them freegrazers Mister Baxter said he was goin' to teach 'em a lesson they'd never forget."

Boss eased up on the muzzle pressure, stepped back, and said, "Get up, you son of a bitch!"

Gus arose clumsily. His ribs were sore. Each deep breath burned like fire. He was still recovering from being hurled against the iron stove in the emporium down at Harmonville.

He was not a large man, more wiry than thick, quick and sinewy rather than strong. He was built like a young man, though he hadn't been young for fifteen years.

Boss went back to the larger man at the head of the riders. He grounded his carbine at a distance of about ten feet and looked the larger man in the eye as he said, "What's your name?"

"Vincent Ballester."

"You ride for Baxter?"

"Yeah."

"How many riders does he have?"

"Seven."

"Where are the other three?"

Vincent Ballester hung fire over his anwer, clearly reluctant to give it. Boss raised the carbine, holding it in both hands like a club.

Charley had listened to their exchange and now was beginning to have a very bad premonition. He addressed Ballester from slightly behind him and to his left. "You're wastin' time, cowboy."

Ballester flinched at the menace in Charley's voice. "They was sent down to that wagoncamp. Are you fellers from down there?"

Neither answered. Boss swung his carbine again, but harder this time. Although Ballester tried to jump away, the blow smashed into his left hip with all the force Boss could put into it, knocking him to the ground. Ballester roiled dust as he flailed his arms, a strangling scream in his throat.

Charley aimed his six-gun at the other two men. They did not seem to be breathing as they watched Ballester writhing in agony. Charley said, "Get belly-down, flat out!"

As Boss stood above the writhing man, face contorted, Charley went over the prone men for weapons, didn't find any, gathered up what weapons they had dropped earlier, shoved them into his britches top, and went among the horses, angrily slashing horsehair cinches. He hoorawed the horses until they went flinging away into the darkness, dumping saddles as they ran.

He went over to Boss and said, "Let's go." He had to repeat it twice before Boss hauled around, leaving the injured man moaning through clenched teeth.

The prone men rolled their eyes to watch their ambushers trot out throught he darkness, but made no move to rise until they heard running horses southward.

Charley did not say a word. Neither did Boss. They had time to guess that even if they could have sprouted wings they would not be able to reach the wagon before Baxter's other three riders had done what they skulked down there to do.

Finally, Charley slackened to a kidney-jolting trot and stood in the stirrups to avoid most of it. They were close enough now to hear gunshots, if there were any. But there weren't, and that made Charley's anxiety increase. It required an effort not to run his horse the rest of the way but a wind-broke horse was not going to contribute anything. Whatever had happened down there had already happened.

Boss swore to himself in a guttural tone. He seemed oblivious of his companion, though he wasn't. When they were almost in sight of the camp he said, "They better be all right or I'm goin' after Baxter, an' when I'm finished with him his own damned mother wouldn't recognize him."

They slackened to a walk. Charley held up a hand. "If it's an ambush . . ."

Boss grudgingly dropped down to a walk also, but the look on his face said clearly that ambush or no ambush, he was unwilling to be very cautious.

There was a great depth of silence up ahead. By the time they could make out the ghostly pale wagon canvas, Charley was ready to dismount, leave his horse, and creep ahead on foot.

Boss followed Waite's example, but was not very

quiet about it. They spread out, approaching the camp from two sides. The moon was high and climbing. It was lopsided and pale gray.

Charley came down toward the wagon from the northwest. Boss was out there on the opposite side. Nothing moved as they approached. Charley took a chance, but knelt to make himself a smaller target as he cupped both hands and called ahead.

"Button? Mose?"

The only sound was his echo.

Charley remained kneeling for a while trying to hold back his bad premonition, which was a sickening dread by now.

Boss called to him in an unsteady voice from the rear of the wagon. "Come on in, Charley."

Boss was standing just outside the texas in moonlight, hands hanging at his sides. The tailgate canvas kept out most of the moonlight, but enough got beneath it to stop Charley Waite in his tracks.

Mose was lying spread out on his back. Button was lying nearby on his side, his head on his arm as though he were sleeping. He had one leg crooked up over the other.

A puddle of glistening blood that looked black in the moonlight spread out beside Mose's head. He had been shot slightly in front of, and slightly above, the ear.

He was beyond help and had been for a couple of hours. If Charley and Boss hadn't been so far northward, they would have been able to hear the gunshot on a quiet night like this one. But they had.

Boss seemed incapable of coming beneath the overhead canvas. He seemed to have been paralyzed by shock.

Charley leaned aside his Winchester, went over beside Mose, saw the swollen, bruised face with its wide-open eyes staring straight upward, and turned toward Button.

He knelt to gently ease the youth onto his back, and Button moaned.

Chapter Seven
Departure of the Sun

Button did not recover consciousness until shortly before dawn. But even then he was incoherent. He had been struck alongside the head above the temple. His hair was matted with dried blood, but he was alive. Charley told Boss that as bad as the swelling looked, unless Button's skull had been cracked he would recover.

Boss knelt beside the bedroll, nodding his head and holding Button's limp hand.

Charley needed time, and because he'd already done everything he knew to do for Button, he took a pick and shovel and walked southward from the wagon to start digging Mose's grave.

He hadn't been in favor of fighting Baxter, or anyone else, at the outset. If he'd been in Boss Spearman's boots he'd have struck camp this morning and started on westward. There was stirrup-high feed out there for many miles. They had all seen it out there.

He dug and sweated, sucked down big gulps of air, and swung the pick until he was past hardpan into moist earth, where all he needed was the shovel.

He'd thought for some time now that what Boss had said was right: the day of the freegrazers was about over and done with.

But last night's raid had changed everything. To stampede the cattle was one thing, maybe to be expected. It certainly had been done before when they'd freegrazed into territory claimed by established ranchers.

But murder was a different matter, especially since there had been no need for it. If the cattle had been stampeded out of the territory, Boss and his crew wouldn't have any choice but to go after them, by which time they would be many miles westward by now.

He paused to lean on the shovel and shake sweat off. It was cold, which he had not noticed. It was also getting close to dawn. He spat on his hands and went back to digging, slamming the shovel into yielding prairie soil as though it were a mortal enemy.

Charley did not have a quick temper, but he did have a temper. It took more to get Charley Waite roiled up than it did most men.

Losing Mosely Harrison was like losing a brother. Big Mose never slackered, never complained, was loyal as they came. He wasn't a deep thinker, but maybe that was in his favor. He joshed a lot and took joshing in good spirit. He sure as hell deserved better than to be shot from hiding like that by some bushwhacker lying out in the darkness. If there was any consolation to his death it had to be that Mose probably hadn't had any idea what happened. A head shot like that killed a man instantly.

"You don't have to go to China," Boss said from the rim of the grave.

Charley held up the shovel. Boss grasped the upper end and braced himself as Charley climbed out, paused to beat moist soil off his legs, and straightened up. The sky was pale gray, which made Boss's face look old. Scraggly gray beard-stubble heightened that impression.

Charley said, "How's Button?"

"He come around after I got a little whiskey down him."

"What did he see?"

"Nothing. Neither of them did until someone out in the night shot Mose, then they charged in, and when Button tried to climb over the tailgate one of 'em hauled him back by the ankles an' another one hit him alongside the head."

"How many?"

Boss answered only after looking steadily at Charley for a moment. "Three."

"Did he see any of their faces?"

"No. It all happened fast after they shot Mose."

Charley groped for his makings and rolled a smoke in silence. He lit up the same way and watched daylight breaking. "We should have moved on," he said.

Boss's reply was short. "We didn't."

Charley blew smoke at the watery gray sky. "We got to hitch up and take Button to that doctor down there. It's not like a busted hip, Boss, like you give that son of a bitch up yonder."

"I wish I'd shot him, Charley."

Waite ignored that. "A bad hit on the head can crack a man's skull and make him strange for the rest of his life." Charley leaned to drop the quirley down into the grave. "Let's bury Mose and go hunt down that doctor."

Putting Mose into his final place of rest did not take long, but shoveling the dirt in did. Afterward when they straggled back to the camp, they made coffee, which was all either of them wanted, before they brought in the team and flung on the harness.

The sun was climbing and it was probably going to be another hot day. But while they loaded the wagon and chained up the tailgate and got untracked in the direction of Harmonville, it was still cool. It remained that way until late afternoon, when they stopped in a bosque of white oaks to set up camp for the night. Then the heat rolled up off the ground as it also came downward from above.

It was pleasant among the oak trees. There was feed for the team first, and when Charley and Boss finally sat down to their evening meal, they were ready to eat.

Button came out of the wagon with dusk arriving. They had done their best for him by soaking the matted hair and cleaning the wound. It was an ugly gash, badly swollen now and hot to the touch, but it was no longer bleeding.

Button sat down very carefully, like a man would who was balancing something atop his head. They offered him supper but he shook his head. "You buried Mose back there?"

Boss replied, "Yes."

"But . . . he didn't get a chance," Button blurted, lips trembling.

Charley kept his eyes on his tin plate. Boss, too, did not look up. Button finally fled out among the trees, where he could lie down and let the tears come.

Boss turned aside to spit out some gristle, turned back, and said, "I'm goin' to settle with Baxter, Charley. I don't give a damn if he's got an army, I'm goin' to see him down on his knees begging."

Charley drank coffee before commenting. "You can have Baxter, Boss. I'm goin' after that town marshal. After him, I'm goin' after whoever else was in that fight at the store, besides Gus."

Boss stopped chewing to eye the younger man. He seemed about to speak, but didn't. Not until they had finished supper and were rolling smokes did he say, "After Baxter, I want the skulking son of a bitch that shot Mose from ambush."

Charley was quiet for a long while. He was watching Button returning from among the oaks when he said, "It might have been better if one of us had gone down there and got that doctor to ride back with us. Harmonville's not real friendly toward us."

Boss snorted. "Damned few towns ever have been."

Button went past them as though they did not exist, climbed over the tailgate, and disappeared inside the wagon. They finished their coffee, their smokes, banked the coals for the breakfast fire, and dragged their bedrolls out a short distance.

Charley fell asleep quickly. Boss lay on his back, thick arms raised, hands beneath his head, looking at the stars.

* * *

The night did not seem long enough to Charley. Even then Boss had meat frying and coffee boiling before he awakened.

Grave digging was something that made a man's muscles ache from the feet upward. It wasn't like other varieties of manual labor that a man could become accustomed to. In a lifetime a man might never dig more than two or three graves. Charley stood up to yank on his britches and tighten his belt. Even one grave was one too many, he told himself, and went over to the wash-basin.

Button had a fever. Boss was worried when he handed Charley his breakfast. "I hope it's just an infection. That'd be bad enough, but if it's from inside his head . . ."

Charley tried to be reassuring. "He talks all right, Boss. He don't fall down when he walks or such things."

They left the bosque of trees shortly ahead of sunrise and by the time the sun began to soar they were moving steadily across open country that neither of them had seen before by daylight. But today there was something new, a cloudbank of enormous white rain galleons bearing down in disarray from the north.

Boss studied them and said, "Maybe by tonight. More likely not until tomorrow." He looked around at the man beside him on the wagon seat. "Seems that whenever it rains in this country it don't horse around about it."

Charley was watching for rooftops. By the time he could distantly make them out, the massive clouds had moved in front of the sun, blotting out daylight. Yet the air did not smell of rain, so Charley thought Boss might be right about when the storm would arrive.

Boss jarred him from a reverie by saying, "If there's lightning and thunder this time, it'll most likely do what Baxter tried to do—stampede our damned cattle to kingdom come."

Charley was watching a solitary horseman riding a short distance north of them, heading back in the direction they had come from. He began to have a feeling of enemies closing in, but the rider threw them a high, casual wave and loped on his way.

Harmonville, like the entire countryside as far, and much farther, than a man could see, was beneath that white overhead mass that had obscured the sun. The town looked a little dingy without sunshine.

They entered from the north, part of a variety of rigs heading in or heading out, including several ranch buck-boards, a couple of light wagons, even a fringe-topped surrey and a big old scarred freight wagon being drawn along by twelve Mexican mules.

They were saved the delay of asking around for the doctor. His cottage was just south of Harmonville's Methodist church, one of the few painted-white structures along Main Street. His sign was nailed to the front of a picket fence.

As they warped in close to the plankwalk where a stud ring was embedded in an unkempt big old tree, Boss said, "He ain't a married man," and looped the lines around the brake handle as he started down.

Charley paused on the opposite side. "Why isn't he married?"

Boss was moving out of sight on the wagon's far

side to let down the tailgate and help Button out when he replied. "Don't see any flowers, do you?"

Some other time Charley would have laughed. Now he met Boss behind the wagon. Between them they got Button over the tailgate. He was sweating profusely even though it was not hot today. In fact, it was beginning to get a little cool.

Their arrival had been noted inside the house. As they steered Button through the little gate and up the walk to the porch, a woman opened the door, drying both hands on an apron. She had chestnut-sorrel hair and brown eyes with flecks of gold in them. She looked to be in her twenties. Neither of the men holding the youth between them paid that much attention to her until they halted on the porch and Boss asked if the doctor was in.

The handsome woman was studying Button when she replied. "No. He had to go set the arm of a boy who fell out of an apple tree, but he'll be back directly. Bring him right on in. What . . . was he kicked by a horse?"

They followed her through a parlor to a severely furnished room where everything had been painted white and which smelled of carbolic acid. Neither of them answered her question until they had helped Button sit on the edge of a hard metal table. He helped as much as he could, but fever was rapidly draining his strength.

The woman approached, looked into one eye, then the other, and said, "Put him flat down, please."

They stood back watching her arrange reflectors and then lean to peer into his ears. Boss said, "Lady, it's not his hearing. He hears real well."

She straightened up and slowly turned. "You are his father?"

"No, ma'am. My name is Spearman. This here is Charley Waite. The kid's name is Button. He rides with us. We got cattle a day's ride from here to the west."

The gold-flecked eyes were fixed on Boss. "Mister Spearman, whatever happened to him could have fractured his skull. I was looking for a sign of blood in his ears."

Boss reddened, removed his hat, and nodded as though he understood perfectly.

She asked a question. "Was it a horse kick?"

"No, ma'am, he got clubbed up alongside the head."

The woman looked from one of them to the other, then turned back toward Button as she said, "How did it happen?"

They told her, and during the recitation the doctor walked into the examination room, nodded all around, put aside a small satchel, and frowned at the youth lying on his table.

The handsome woman stepped away to make room for the doctor. As he was examining Button she repeated what she had been told about his injury, in a voice as flat and inflectionless as though she were without human feelings.

The doctor was a rumpled-looking man, beginning to gray at the temples but with an otherwise youthful bearing and appearance. He eyed Boss and Charley in thought before saying, "By any chance, is there another man working for you, a large, powerful man named Mose something-or-other?"

Boss nodded woodenly. "There was. Someone shot him in the head night before last an' we buried him out yonder yesterday morning." Boss jutted his chin toward Button. "That happened the same time someone tried to brain the kid."

For a long moment the only sound in the room was of roadway traffic. The doctor shot a fleeting look in the direction of the woman with the gold-flecked eyes. "You have any idea who did this, Mister—?"

"Spearman. Boss Spearman. Yes, we got an idea who done it. The same men who ganged up on Mose here in town a few days back. . . . I guess you'll be the doctor who bandaged his head."

The man nodded slowly. "Yes. I'm Doctor Barlow." He turned, glanced once more at the handsome woman, then leaned over Button again as the woman herded Boss and Charley out to the parlor, and left them to return to the examination room.

Chapter Eight

A Not Exactly Unexpected Event

It was a long half hour before Doctor Barlow came to the parlor, looking grave. He sat down and pushed his legs out before saying, "It's not a fracture, although I don't know why it isn't because that was quite a blow. It's not an infection either, as close as I can tell now." He eyed Boss and Charley. "My sister has a notion it's something emotional." Doctor Barlow smiled a little apologetically. "Women get odd ideas sometimes."

Boss was scowling. "What are you talkin' about, the fever?"

Doctor Barlow's smile faded. "Yes, the fever. I should have said that first, shouldn't I?"

Boss's perplexed scowl did not leave. "I don't know but what your sister might be right," he said. "The kid's had a hard life an' he was close to Mose. I know Mose's killin' bothered him because he don't seem to have thought of anything else. Of course, it only happened day before yesterday but even so . . . And he got hit alongside the head too. So maybe your sister is right."

Doctor Barlow eyed Spearman through a moment of silence, then slapped his upper legs and shot up to his feet as he said, "He ought to stay here for a few days, Mister Spearman, so we can watch him."

Boss nodded as he was getting to his feet, holding his hat to one side. "That'd be fine with us, doctor. You do whatever's best for him."

"Mister Spearman?"

"Yes."

"Early this morning I had two patients. One with a broken hip, the other with internal injuries to his back and two broken ribs from being hit by someone swinging a Winchester like a maul."

Neither Boss nor Charley said anything. They returned the doctor's gaze without blinking as they put on their hats as though to depart.

Walt Barlow wasn't finished. "According to the man they work for, his two riders were beaten night before last, which would be the same time your man was killed and the boy was injured. . . . Mister Spearman, what I'd like to get settled in my own mind is—which happened first, the beatings or the killing?"

Boss looked at Charley, who answered the doctor. "They must have happened at about the same time. Maybe the attack on our wagoncamp was a little earlier, but I wouldn't want to swear to that. Boss an' I went up north to catch Baxter's riders comin' down to stampede our cattle. We caught them."

Doctor Barlow nodded slowly. "Yes, I'd say you

caught them, from the stories they told me this morning."

Charley ignored the interruption. "Then Boss and I headed for the wagon. By the time we got down there, it was all over. Mose was dead and Button—we thought he was dead too. Doctor, I think maybe those other Baxter riders ambushed Mose and Button before we had a run at those other sons of bitches. Otherwise I think we'd have heard the shot that killed Mose. We'd have heard it if we hadn't been way to hell and gone up north out of hearin' distance waitin' to pull off our ambush."

Doctor Barlow seemed to be balancing all that he had heard from Spearman and Waite against what he had heard from others about these matters. He went out onto the porch with them and asked where they would be if he had to contact them about the boy.

Boss was looking thoughtfully out at the wagon when he replied. He did not have to look up to know a storm was coming. The smell of it was in the air. Also, there was electricity in the manes and tails of his horses out yonder under the big old shaggy tree. If this one was like the last one and they drove the wagon back out where they'd buried Mose, they would be unable to drive to Harmonville and no one from there would be able to ride out to their camp until the ground firmed up again.

He said, "I think we'll go down to the lower end of town, out behind the public corrals maybe, and set up camp down there."

Doctor Barlow nodded and watched them go down to the wagon and head southward down Main Street. His sister came out to stand nearby, watching the battered old wagon as she said, "Why are they going south if their camp is northwest?"

"Because they're going to set up down at the lower end of town to be near the lad."

The handsome woman looked at her brother. "Did you tell them what Denton Baxter said?"

"No."

"Walt! Why didn't you?"

Doctor Barlow answered with spirit. "Because about half the time Dent Baxter is full of bull. Also, because when we'd done what we could for his men he took them back to the ranch with him." Barlow pointed upward. "If those clouds open up, Sue, Baxter won't be able to get back to Harmonville for a week. By then I hope we have the lad able to travel with his friends." He paused. "Sue?"

"Yes?"

"Did you hear what they said about the one called Mose that I patched up a few days back?"

"I heard them say he was dead."

"Shot in the head on a dark night by a bushwhacker out a ways from their camp. Murder, Sue, pure and simple murder, if what Mister Spearman said is true."

Sue Barlow turned from watching the old wagon at the same moment several very fat raindrops struck the steps just beyond the porch overhang. Out in the roadway when large raindrops landed, dust blew upward in miniature clouds.

She entered the house ahead of her brother and went straight on through to the kitchen to fire up the stove. She did not have a single doubt that they were in for another summertime gully washer. As she got the fire started she thought of those two beard-stubbled, weathered men in their runover boots and faded trousers parking their wagon at the lower end of town before the storm arrived.

When she returned to the front of the house the raindrops were beginning to make a cacophony of sound on the roof with long intervals between raindrops. But the intervals grew shorter until, when she lighted a lamp to take into the examination room for her brother, the downpour was making a steady drumroll sound that filled the house, driving people out of the roadway seeking shelter anywhere they could, and within fifteen minutes had turned Main Street into a chocolatey millrace.

A half hour after the first raindrops, Harmonville's plank-walks were deserted. Even tethered horses had been led to shelter. Several stores had lighted lamps in their windows. It would have been possible to fire a cannon from the north end of town through the lower end and not hit a living soul. Also, as the force of the storm increased, it was probable that anyone listening at the lower end of town would not have been able to hear the cannon being fired.

Charley Waite made the dash in a sliding run from the livery barn runway to the wagon after arranging for the care of their team horses. Inside, Boss was eyeing a place where waterproofed canvas rubbing against an ash bow was leaking drops of water. He ignored Charley's swift entrance to put a pan where the drops were falling on their bedrolls.

When he turned and yelled above the noise to ask if Charley had seen the forked lightning, Charley yelled back that he'd been inside the livery barn and hadn't seen anything but water.

Boss gestured northwesterly. "About thirty, forty miles out yonder."

Charley shook his head in understanding without trying to comment above the roar of the rainfall. Thirty, forty miles northwest would be just about where the cattle were. Sometimes thunder by itself did not do it, but lightning never failed to do it—stampede cattle that were half wild anyway.

He sank down amid the boxes and bedding to roll a smoke. He did not speculate on the fact that everything seemed to be coming unraveled, because the few times in his life when things didn't seem that way were very shortly overcome by things that did seem that way. To Charley Waite, Boss Spearman, and most other men and women who lived against the ground, there was Christmastime followed by eleven months when it wasn't Christmastime. They spent those eleven months wearing tin beaks and getting down to scratch to stay alive with the chickens.

Boss came over and dropped down on a rolled set of bedding covered on the outside by a stained, dirty canvas ground cloth. He held out his hands to examine them as he yelled above the noise. "We're going to be stuck here, Charley. I hadn't figured on that. It's not a friendly town toward us."

Charley leaned to tip ash out past the little hole in the tailgate canvas where the covering had been snugged taut by its pucker string. His hand was thoroughly wet when he drew it back, but he'd protected the rice-paper cigarette in his palm. He examined it to be certain it was still lighted when he replied. "Friendly or not, Boss, like you said, we're stuck here." Charley took down a final drag off his smoke and pitched it out into the millrace of the alleyway. "Until this lets up, folks aren't goin' to be thinkin' of much else."

Boss looked at the drip pan. It was not even half full yet. Dampness and a slight chill were inside the wagon with them. He went forward to pull the pucker string, where an occasional little wind was forcing rain over the driving seat up front. Until now there had been no wind, just water coming straight down.

They could have used some light because although it was not yet dusk, it was getting steadily darker inside the wagon.

Charley got comfortable among the bedrolls. Boss rolled their saddleguns in some flour sacks, less to keep them from being dripped on than to absorb the moisture that always filled the air even in dry places during this kind of storm.

He crawled back where Charley was lying with his eyes half closed listening for even the faintest sound of a change in the downpour. Boss settled and said, "Them clouds reached from here to beyond the mountains. I got a feelin' this one's goin' to be worse than that other one."

Charley smiled a little and said something that made it seem he had not heard Boss. "Baxter's got some crippled-up hands."

Boss's response dripped with sulfurous sarcasm. "That's sure too bad. An' him being such an upstandin' citizen and all."

Charley continued to smile, very faintly. "One with a busted hip. I didn't know you hit him that hard."

"I hit the son of a bitch as hard as I could!"

"And that scrawny one named Gus. Two broken ribs and some bruises around back." Charley twisted to look at the older man. "There was another pair. Mose said he broke the arm of one and smashed the face of another one. Boss, if all them things happened to Baxter's riders, how could he still have four to get ambushed by us and another three to raid the camp?"

Boss was punching blankets to get more comfortable when he replied. "Nobody said they all rode for Baxter. Them four we overhauled did but no one said the others had to. Not that I heard anyway."

Charley went back to squinting past the pucker hole in the tailgate canvas, where rooftops over across Main Street appeared as vague as though they were fifty miles away behind a blanket of wood smoke.

The gloom increased, the downpour did not slacken, and by the time they were hungry Boss made a statement that pretty well summed up their situation. "We better go over to the cafe. We'd get drowned tryin' to make a cookin' fire outside."

There were four rubber ponchos in the wagon. One had belonged to Mose; it was big enough to house two men. Another one had been patched with pitch; it belonged to Button. They stood up to remove their hats and pull the other two over their heads and were ready.

Outside, rain darkened their hats before they got across the alley to walk up through the shadowy livery barn runway to the front roadway. Up there, they halted to watch runnels of water coursing southward, in places as wide as creeks.

Northward, a man holding a canvas above his head was wading through mud above his ankles to reach the opposite duckboards. They watched his progress. Behind them that scarecrow of a hostler with the milky eyes came up without even a coat. He leaned with a cupped hand to yell to Charley. "If it don't quit it'll wash the damned town away."

Charley nodded, watching that wet figure up north reach the far plankwalk, lower his canvas, and shake like a dog before ducking into a store.

Boss removed his old hat, punched it from the inside until the crown resembled a tipi, reset it, and yelled at Charley. "Let's go."

Water swirled up over their boottops in a particularly deep washout they did not know was out there. Feeling cold water around their toes was of less concern than groping ahead a foot at a time to feel for another washout.

The water's force was sweeping a slab-sided mongrel dog around and around as he foolishly tried to swim against the current. Boss saw the dog being inexorably tumbled toward them, braced thick legs wide, and leaned with both hands as the terrified dog came past. He got two grips on a skinny back, and as the dog yelped, Boss swung him out of the water and began forcing his passage toward the opposite storefront.

Charley used Boss's pathway as his own. Once they both were nearly swept off their feet where a sunken hole had created a small but powerful whirl of brown water.

Someone's shout of encouragement was swept away by a rising wind. If they heard the shout they did not look up to see where it had come from.

Boss almost went to his knees, still clutching the dog. Charley pushed past, got an arm around an overhang upright in front of the general store, stepped back, and threw out his free hand. Boss grabbed it in a viselike grip and Charley used the leverage of the upright to pull his companion the final five feet to safety on the plankwalk.

Boss shook his head and laughed. Charley pushed him away from the swirling water, which was within inches of overflowing the duckboards, then removed his hat to dump water and to run a soaked hand down over his face to push off more water.

Boss leaned to put the dog down as a large man emerged from the general store to grab the dog before it could flee, even though it did not appear to have flight in mind. It was shaking like a leaf, too frightened to do anything but cower at Boss's feet.

The big man lifted the dog and yelled at Boss. "I owe you, mister. It's my daughter's pup. I tried to grab it up in front of the harness shop but the water was too fast for me." The big man shoved out a wet hand, which Boss gripped and then turned to yell at Charley. "You all right?"

Charley was wiping his dripping nose when he answered. "Never felt better in my life. Where is that damned cafe?"

Chapter Nine
Butler!

It could have been suppertime. It was dark enough to be, but in fact was midafternoon. Even so, the cafe counter was full of men talking at the top of their lungs, every one of them wearing clothing darkened by the wet.

The cafeman was as busy as a cat in a sandbox and did not look up as the latest arrivals looked for places to sit. At the lower end of the counter two burly, bearded freighters pushed left and right to make places and beckoned. They were rough, loud men with trousers wet above the knees and mud caked on their boots. One of them leaned as Charley sat down and said, "You ever see so much damned water come down in an hour before in your life?"

Charley shook his head. "Never did. What I'd like to know is when it'll let up."

The freighter reached for a crockery mug of

coffee. "From the looks of the sky, maybe not for a week." He drank noisily and lowered the cup to look at Charley and Boss. "If you fellers is passin' through, you'd better hole up at the rooming-house before all the beds are gone."

The cafeman arrived looking harassed. They ordered whatever he had that was hot. The cafeman nodded brusquely and hastened away.

The freighter on Boss's right leaned on the counter with thick arms and said, "It's not a regular storm or there'd be thunder an' lightning. This here is more like that one that washed away Gunnison up north ten, twelve years ago. Water come down that damned canyon carrying melted snow until it was about twenty feet high with nowhere to go but straight into town. Killed a lot of people."

Men left the cafe leaving mud behind as more men pushed in out of the darkening day. The cafeman took time out from fetching food to light a pair of lamps on his pie table. Every time someone opened the roadway door the lamps would wildly flicker.

The freighters finished their meal and were rising to pay up and depart when another large, thick man walked in and came down the counter. He saw Charley and Boss, smiled from ear to ear, and slapped each of them resoundingly on the back as one of the rising freighters said, "Did you catch her dog, Mack?"

The man addressed as Mack jutted his jaw downward. "This gent did. He was wading the roadway. The pup come in front and he grabbed it."

The three big freighters showed approval of Boss's presence of mind by rapping him across the shoulders as they headed for the door.

The downpour did not slacken. If anything, it seemed to be coming down harder. It certainly was making more noise. Boss and Charley concentrated on the first cafe-cooked meal either of them had eaten in a long time. Even the coffee tasted better than camp coffee.

Gradually the other diners thinned out. The cafeman got a little respite and used it to amble down the counter to lean on his pie table opposite Spearman and Waite and carve off a cud of tobacco as he loudly said, "There's worse things than being stranded in Harmonville."

Boss looked up. "Name one, mister."

The cafeman took it as a joke and grinned, got his cud tucked into his cheek, and went after the coffeepot to refill their cups.

Another customer stamped in out of the darkening day. The cafeman looked up from pouring coffee and called out a cheerful greeting. "Nice day, marshal."

Neither of the freegrazers raised his head nor altered the rhythm of his chewing, but both sat stone-still for a moment.

The cafeman went up where Marshal Poole had dropped down on the damp counter bench. Evidently Marshal Poole had not looked at the other diners. He said, "Meat'n spuds like always, Les, and coffee. It's worth a man's life to cross the road."

The cafeman was sympathetic. "I know it is. Potholes two feet deep out there. But it'll stop. It always has, hasn't it?"

Al Poole did not answer. He was leaning slightly to see around the diners between himself and down where the freegrazers were eating. He very slowly straightened back, picked up his coffee cup when it arrived, using both hands, and sipped very slowly.

There was less loud talk now as fewer diners concentrated on eating, but the other noise overhead and outside did not diminish at all.

Boss pushed his platter away, leaned back to dig for silver in a trouser pocket, and made a point of not turning his head.

When Charley was also finished they arose and headed for the door, deliberately ignoring everything on their right. They almost made it. Marshal Poole called to them. He too was standing, but he was straddling the counter bench. They faced around as Marshal Poole said, "I'd like a few words with you gents."

Boss nodded woodenly. "We'll be outside." He opened the door and closed it behind Charley. Marshal Poole was still watching them as they moved toward the edge of the plank-walk to consider the drowning town and countryside. Charley spoke with his back to the cafe. "Sure as hell Baxter talked to him this morning when he brought in his casualties."

Boss nodded, sucked his teeth, and expectorated into the rising roadway millrace. "Yeah."

Two women in voluminous skirts that were wet halfway to their knees went northward holding their bonnets. The intermittent whipping wind that had been blowing earlier had now become a constant irritation.

Charley said, "Unless I miss my guess, Boss, he's not going to want to hear our side of it."

Boss spat again. "He's goin' to, though, whether he wants to or not."

"When was the last time you got locked inside a jailhouse, Boss?"

Spearman turned his head. "A month or such a matter before I left Texas. You?"

"Never have been and I'm not really lookin' forward to it this time. Not in Denton Baxter's town."

Marshal Poole emerged from the cafe pulling his hat down hard as the wind picked up a little. He was working a toothpick with his left hand as he walked over and eyed the roadway. Without facing the other men or using any preliminary he said, "Mister Baxter swore out a warrant for you two this morning."

Boss, taking his cue from the lawman, also faced the roadway. "For what?"

"Attempted murder. Four of his riders identified both of you as the ambushers who waylaid them night before last and beat hell out of his foreman and one of his riders." Finally, Poole spat out the toothpick and twisted from the waist.

Boss met his stare. "We'd like to swear out a warrant too, marshal. That big feller you had in your cells . . . someone shot him from out in the dark without any warning and tried to brain the kid who rides with us."

"You saw them do that, did you?"

Boss shook his head without explaining why he and Charley had not seen the murder. "The boy survived. After they killed Mose they came into camp, tried to kill him too."

Poole looked thoughtful. "Where is the boy?"

"Up at the doctor's house. I guess they thought they'd killed him too. They almost did."

Marshal Poole turned back to gazing into the roadway. "I'll go talk to him after I lock you two up."

Boss slowly shook his head at the lawman. "I don't think so, Mister Poole. You don't lock nobody up unless you serve our warrant on Baxter and fetch him in to be locked up too. And you don't go near the boy. He's sicker'n a dog. No one's goin' to badger him. No one." Boss met the lawman's steady gaze with one just as steady. "While you're about it, marshal, you might want to bring in a rider called Gus. Him and that big feller with the busted hip didn't make no secret about Baxter sendin' them out to stampede our cattle. They also told us where the other men were—down south to raid our camp. One of those three is a murderer. The other two were with him. One of them tried to brain the boy."

Marshal Poole said, "You camping here in town?"

Boss nodded. "Got our wagon out behind the livery barn."

Poole nodded his head. "All right. You won't be leaving for a while. But you're plumb welcome to try. Meanwhile I'm goin to round up some possemen, and if I got to smoke you out of your wagon, believe me, Mister Spearman, I'll do it."

Marshal Poole stepped down into the swirling tide of swift-racing roadway water and began groping his way toward the other side. Charley and Boss watched his progress. When Poole finally reached the opposite side he did not turn toward his jailhouse office, but northward in the direction of Doctor Barlow's place. Boss swore and lunged out into the roadway with Charley behind him. Boss's anger made him careless. Once he fell into a washout and got pretty well soaked before Charley helped him up. He struck out again as though nothing had happened, reached the opposite plank-walk in front of the poolhall, and struck out swiftly to overtake the marshal. Charley had to stretch out to keep up and even then was unable to match Boss's stride until they were at the little picket fence outside the doctor's cottage.

Marshal Poole was already on the porch raising his fist to knock, when Boss bellowed at him and whipped up the right side of his poncho.

Poole twisted at the precise moment the door opened behind him and the handsome woman stood in the opening. Charley held his breath. Boss couldn't fire first because the woman would be directly in his line of fire. If Poole went for his gun, Boss was going to be killed.

Charley moved swiftly in front of Boss as he called to the lawman. "Get away from the door!"

Poole did not move. Behind him the handsome woman did, though; she took one forward step and bumped Marshal Poole with her shoulder. He was not standing squarely on his feet. He had to fling out both arms to keep his balance.

Boss covered the intervening distance swiftly. The woman ignored him to face Poole's anger. He was struggling to say something when Boss arrived at the foot of the stairs and bellowed at him. "I told you to stay away from the kid!"

The woman glanced briefly at Boss's darkly angry features before returning her attention to Marshal Poole. She smiled sweetly at him. "Excuse me, marshal. The porch is wet and I slipped." She paused, then spoke again. "You want to see the boy who was hurt the other night?" Before Marshal Poole could reply she gently shook her head at him. "I'm afraid that's not possible. My brother gave him an injection to make him sleep. He probably won't awaken until tomorrow morning."

The lawman was red in the face. He glared at the woman, still groping for something to say. Charley moved aside so the steps would be unobstructed. At their bottom, Boss still stood like a rooted oak, right hand beneath the drooping folds of his poncho.

The woman's tawny eyes were perfectly calm as she said, "There's hot coffee inside, marshal, if you'd care to come in and wait for my brother."

Poole turned his back on her, stamped down the steps, and did not look back even after he had cleared the picket fence and was walking southward under the full force of the storm. He probably did not even feel the water.

Boss let his right hand hang as he studied the handsome woman. "Lady, don't ever do anything like that again."

She gave Boss the same sweet smile. "Come up here out of the rain, Mister Spearman." She smiled at Charley and moved toward the doorway. After Boss and Charley had dropped their ponchos and entered the house, the woman led them through to a warm, dry kitchen that smelled of freshly baked bread. She pointed to chairs at an old scrubbed table, then went after coffee cups.

They watched everything she did.

When she brought their coffee she said, "My brother was called out an hour or so ago. Would either of you care for fresh cream?"

Neither one of them did. They dropped soggy hats to the floor and hunched around the hot cups gazing at her. Eventually Charley put a hand to his forehead and gently shook his head from side to side.

She smiled at him. "Mister Waite, yelling at him wouldn't have done any good."

That was probably true, but bumping into him when he and Boss were a hairsbreadth from shooting was as close as she would ever come in this lifetime to getting shot.

Boss threw himself against the back of the chair, looking at her. "How's Button, ma'am?"

Her smile faded. She looked into the cup she was holding. She did not have to speak; the change was noticeable to both men. Boss said, "Worse?"

She did not look up when she replied. "No better, Mister Spearman. The fever is burning him up. We tried cold rags without any luck at all." She finally raised her eyes to them. "He has periods of delirium when he talks about everything under the sun. Do either of you know a man named Butler? I think he has a broken arm. My brother set a broken arm for a man he'd never seen before last week."

Boss shook his head, but Charley's eyes narrowed a little. "Butler . . . Boss, one of those men Mose beat in the store got his arm broken. Lady, what about Butler?"

"Button said the name several times. He seemed to be saying a man named Butler was trying to pull him off the tailgate of a wagon with one arm yelling to someone to help him."

Charley stared at Boss Spearman. "He *did* see them. I know what he told us; he didn't see them. But he did and he heard a name. Boss, one of those fellers who jumped Mose at the store got a broken arm." Charley leaned to pick up his hat before arising. "The storekeeper where they had the fight might know the name of the man who got his arm busted."

Sue did not try to delay them. She went out where they shrugged into their ponchos and looked at the leaden, low sky as she said, "I'll tell Walt you were here. He'll be interested."

Chapter Ten
No Letup

The downpour still had not slackened. There was every indication that it wouldn't for a long time as Charley and Boss stood on the edge of the west-side plankwalk trying to guess from eddying dark whirlpools exactly where the deepest washouts were.

On the opposite side of the road several loafers were standing beneath a leaky wooden overhang out front of the abstract office, watching Spear-man and Waite. One cupped his hands, yelled, then gestured. Charley waved back and stepped down into the water. Its force was greater than he'd expected. He had to lean and grab an up-right until his feet were braced, then he cautiously started forward.

The loafers moved across the flooded duck-boards to watch as Boss also stepped down. He had seen Charley's close call and clung to the overhang upright until he was ready to start ahead.

They were unable to cross directly toward the watchers; the torrent was too strong, so they angled southward and were midway across when a shout from the loafers made them stop and turn. Coming into town from the north was a stagecoach whose driver was standing up trying to line out his four-horse hitch so as to avoid the most obvious whirlpools.

The driver was holding his hitch to a slow walk. The horses had the water's force behind them. Because they sensed danger, they were feeling their way. A hundred yards southward men were standing out front of the corralyard office. They were the yardmen and the manager of the stage company.

Boss yelled above the noise of the downpour. "Let 'em pass, Charley."

Waite was already past the center of the road and would have to back up to do this. He watched the big stage for a moment, then risked two long steps forward so the coach could pass between them.

The driver saw them but gave no sign of it. His only interest at the moment was avoiding two-foot-deep washouts. If his horses did not step into such a hole, one or two of his coach wheels might. If that occurred it was very possible his stage would go over on its side.

There were passengers leaning out on both sides, getting drenched, but because they recognized the more immediate danger of capsizing, they were ignoring the water.

The whip was a short, wiry man wearing a poncho over a coat. He looked twice as broad as he actually was. Charley saw the man's right cheek bulging from a cud of tobacco.

Boss halted, legs spread. Opposite him with room enough for the coach to pass between them, Charley was turning back by inching one foot at a time, feeling for sound footing. The thoroughly engrossed loafers were like statues on the eastside plankwalk.

The offside lead horse was a high-headed, big, powerful beast who was probably bay but right now looked either dark brown or black. His nostrils were distended as he felt his way ahead with both eyes bulging.

He was not watching the water. None of the horses were; they were concentrating on their footing. Dead ahead of the bug-eyed big leader was a whirlpool. Charley cupped his hands to yell to the driver to haul to the right. The driver either did not hear him or did not see the whirlpool. He was feeling the temperament of his horses through the lines and squinting over their heads in the direction of the corralyard.

Charley yelled again. This time the whip flicked him a glance, then ignored him to peer straight ahead from beneath his droopy hat brim. He did not have much farther to go, about a hundred yards.

Charley saw the high-headed horse batting his eyes to clear them of rainwater. The damned fool was going to step straight into that whirlpool, which was bad enough, but if the offside forewheel went down into it too the coach would very likely tip over, and Charley was right where this would happen.

He had a moment to recognize his peril and to realize that he could not turn to flee toward the loafers because swift, frantic movement would send him sprawling in the millrace, where the coach would crush him.

He moved his invisible feet back around facing the east side of the roadway, prayed the current would not upset him, and when it didn't he raised both arms from beneath the poncho and lunged for the head of the offside leader, caught leather, and flung all his weight into an effort to force the horse's head away from him.

The driver screamed a string of profanity and leaned to brace as the leader forced his harness mate to stagger to the right. Boss had to flounder backward on the far side to avoid having steel tires grind over his feet. He fell backward, swearing and floundering.

Charley put all his weight and strength into forcing the leaders away from the whirlpool. He stepped into it himself and lost his footing but clung to the big horse and was pulled out of a deep hole to more solid footing.

The coach missed the whirlpool by about ten inches. Boss was on all fours scrambling back the way he had come to get well clear of the wheels.

Charley braced, got his feet set, then released the big horse and pushed as the coach passed him. He met a grizzled man's bulging stare, then the rig was on southward almost to the corralyard gates and Boss was struggling up out of the mud.

The loafers cheered as Charley reached a hand to Boss and pulled him close so they could continue to the east plankwalk by helping each other.

The loafers leaned, grabbed both men, and hauled them onto the sidewalk, now under about three inches of water.

Boss pushed away, moved toward the building,

and glared at Charley. "What in the hell were you trying to do?"

Before Waite could answer, one of the loafers waved his arm in the direction of the sluggish whirlpool. "He pushed that high-headed leader to the other side. You see that damned hole out where the water's boilin' round and round?"

Boss wiped his face, went closer, saw the whirlpool, and blew out a ragged loud breath. He roughly nudged Charley and struck out southward in the direction of the general store.

Behind them the loafers watched their departure while excitedly talking among themselves. One man said, "He had to do it, or otherwise when a wheel went down in there the damned stage would sure as hell have tipped over on him." Another man said, "Yeah. All right. And just how many men do you know who'd figure things fast enough to do what he done? An' I'll tell you something else: if that coach had tipped over, them passengers would have got hurt. Maybe the leader would have busted his legs too."

The former speaker made a proposal. "Let's go down to the saloon." The loafers agreed.

Down at the corralyard the onlookers watched Spearman and Waite enter the general store before turning to enter the corralyard, where a white-faced driver and his badly shaken passengers were hunching against the rain.

The emporium was empty of customers. There were three ceiling lamps giving off orangey light while the proprietor and a youthful clerk stood side by side at the front window gazing out. They had just finished sandbagging the doorway entrance.

When Boss and Charley walked in, shiny black

in their ponchos, with water still running steadily off the trough of their hat brims, the proprietor turned with a strained smile. He had heard the shouting up toward the north end of town and risked going out front to stand beneath his wooden overhang to watch the episode with the stagecoach.

He beckoned them deeper into his large old building with its laden shelves and oiled floor, over where a small iron stove was popping. He was a balding, thin man wearing sleeve protectors and a short cloth apron. He fished behind a counter, produced two fat cigars, and handed them over. "Them stage passengers'd likely do better. They sure owe you boys. So does Barry. He's got the stage franchise. You saved him a busted coach, maybe some horses he'd have had to shoot, and some damned mad travelers. Now then, what can I do for you?"

Boss and Charley lighted their stogies over the mantle of a counter lamp before answering. The cigars were mellow and delightfully fragrant. While Charley was studying his with interest—although he'd smoked stogies before, he'd never in his life smoked one with this kind of quality—Boss answered the storekeeper's question.

"There was a fight in here a week or so ago. Some range-men jumped a big feller with scars on his face."

The storekeeper's smile faded. Though caution showed in his gaze now, he did not fidget. He leaned on his counter, nodding. "Yes. What about it?"

"There was a feller got an arm broken."

The storekeeper nodded again. "Yes. What about him?"

"What is his name?"

Charley stared at the storekeeper. So did Boss. The man would have had to be simpleminded not to suspect that the pair of wet, muddy, beard-stubbled, thoroughly disreputable looking men gazing at him had a reason for asking their question.

He straightened up off the counter, shot a glance up front where his youthful clerk was watching water rising up the sandbags, sighed, and said, "Ed Butler. What about him?"

"You know him?"

"Yes. He's been around since last autumn. Rides for Mister Baxter, who ranches up—"

"Is he Mister Baxter's range boss, maybe?"

"Oh no. That'd be Vince Ballester. He's a bigger and heavier man than Butler. No, I'd say that maybe Butler's a troubleshooter for Mister Baxter. He's usually got one or two like that on his payroll. He's had trouble with free . . ."

"Go on, friend. With freegrazers?"

The storekeeper smiled and offered a little apologetic palms-up gesture with both hands. "No offense, gents."

Boss smiled back. "Sure not, friend."

The storekeeper considered them cautiously. "I'd like to ask a question. . . ."

"Go right ahead," replied Boss, plugging the expensive stogie back into his mouth.

"Well, that big feller who drubbed hell out of those three. He got hit over the head pretty hard when Marshal Poole slipped up behind him. Is he all right?"

Boss removed the stogie to look at it as he replied, "He's dead, mister. A few nights back someone snuck up in the darkness and shot him in the head."

The storekeeper's eyes widened on Boss, then went off to one side to watch the clerk up front trying to keep water out. Boss said, "We're much obliged for the cigars. They're the best I ever smoked."

He and Charley were turning away when the storekeeper called them back. "Wait a minute. Here, have two more."

They accepted the cigars and stored them very carefully in shirt pockets where they would be protected and dry, as the storekeeper leaned on the counter to say, "Gents, I'd take it kindly if you'd never mention bein' in here and us talkin'."

Boss was agreeable. "Not a word about you, mister."

They had to step over sandbags to reach the roadway. By now it was impossible to tell where the road ended and the board sidewalks began. The storekeeper was not the only one employing sandbags. Up and down Main Street on both sides men were creating barriers to keep water from their business establishments.

Charley looked over in the direction of the jailhouse. Although the distance was not great, it was like looking through a heavy fog. There was a faint light showing in the window. He smoked his stogie and followed Boss northward. When they fetched up outside of the saloon where about a dozen loafers were leaning against the building protected by an old wooden overhang awning that leaked everywhere men were not standing, Boss said, "What're you holding your hat like that for?"

"Because I don't want water on my cigar."

When they entered expecting to find the saloon at least partially full, since there was damned little that men could do in this kind of weather but drink and swap lies, they were surprised to find only three townsmen along the bar and the proprietor with his titty-pink ruffled sleeve garters reading a newspaper with the help of a counter lamp. He looked up at them, stared a moment or two, folded his newspaper, pushed it under the bartop, and went to meet them. He had the expression of someone who knows exactly who is standing across from him.

Charley said, "Whiskey."

As the barman turned away, Charley shrugged at Boss. "Do freegrazers smell different?"

Boss did not answer because the barman was back with a bottle and two glasses. He said, "On the house, gents." They stared at him, so he explained. "I saw you keep that dumb horse from steppin' into the hole a while back. I'm not sure I'd have tried it." He nodded toward the bottle. "As much as you want," he told them and went back down where the little lamp was and fished around for his newspaper.

Boss filled both shot glasses with a steady hand, but made no move to hoist his until he'd put a sardonic smile on his companion. "Strange how a man comes up a hero when all he's tryin' to do is keep from being squashed, ain't it?"

Charley lifted the little glass. "I'm gettin' a taste for it, Boss. Shall we light up those other two stogies to go with the whiskey?"

"Naw. Too soon. We ought to treasure them. Maybe smoke them when the storm lets up."

"They might get soggy by then."

Boss tipped his head, raised the glass and

dropped the whiskey straight down, then he braced. But nothing happened; no water filled his eyes, his throat did not burn, his stomach did not squinch up.

He lowered his head, watching Charley licking his lips, and reached to twist the bottle until he could see the label.

"Charley?"

"What."

"Read the label."

Charley read it. "Imported Irish Whiskey." He tilted the bottle very carefully to refill his glass.

Chapter Eleven
Another Crossing

They ate supper in an atmosphere of damp clothing, smelly roadway mud, and the same monotonous racket made by the undiminished downpour they'd been living with since the storm had arrived.

There was almost no conversation among the other diners. Charley got the feeling that the storm was wearing thin a lot of nerves in Harmonville. Personally, he was philosophical about it. When it was time, it would stop. Until it was time, it would not. He leaned toward Boss and said, "We got to cross that damned roadway again."

Spearman answered around a cheekful of food. "I been wonderin' where the marshal an' his vigilantes are. When he left the doctor's porch he looked mad enough to chew nails and spit rust." Boss swallowed with the aid of a mouthful of coffee, then said, "I'll tell you something, Charley. If it wasn't for this storm we'd have had Baxter an' the marshal down our throats by now, an' we wouldn't have learned as much as we have."

The cafeman came to refill their cups and go among his other diners to repeat the process. He neither smiled nor spoke. Charley watched him retreat back behind the big flowered curtain that separated his counter from the cooking area, and he wondered if the cafeman wasn't also getting cabin fever from being cooped up by the storm.

Boss jarred him by saying, "Why don't someone string a rope across the roadway? If this keeps up won't anybody be able to cross over without one by tomorrow."

A gaunt man wearing a waterproof coat looked at Boss. "That's a good idea," he said, and shoved out a bony hand. "I'm Ed Garnet the harness maker."

Boss gripped the harness maker's hand and released it. "I'm Boss Spearman. This here is Charley Waite."

Ed Garnet's eyes narrowed perceptibly, which Boss noticed and said, "Freegrazers, Mister Garnet. Want to take that handshake back?"

The harness maker arose, put some silver beside his empty plate, nodded without speaking, and left the cafe. Boss shrugged and went back to his meal. "These folks could be six feet under water with us holdin' out a rope to 'em and they wouldn't take it."

They were the last diners to leave the cafe. Behind them the cafeman closed and locked his door and went after more towels to push against the bottom of the door from the inside.

They were solemnly considering the roadway,

which had a slight crest to the dark water toward the center, when an old man passed by, guessed their intention, and said, "Ain't safe, boys. You can still make it down to the roominghouse though." He waited for a response, which was not forthcoming, and also said, "Back in 'sixty-nine it was almost this bad. Damned rain didn't let up for a week. Folks was diggin' out until Christmastime."

Boss gripped an overhang post and tested the water for depth. Close to the sidewalk the force was less than it was farther out. He swore with feeling and groped with his other boot.

What added to the danger was increasing darkness. They had to lean against the current and move inches at a time. Without raising his eyes from the water he yelled back over his shoulder. "I'm goin' to leave this damned country as soon as Button can travel and we can find the cattle, and don't ever want to hear about it again as long as I live."

Charley saw him abruptly disappear to his waist about five feet ahead. He stopped dead still, leaning northward. Boss flailed with both arms beneath the poncho, which was no longer able to perform its designated function, and hadn't been able to since the last time Boss had fallen. He looked like a large black bird with shiny black wings as he beat the air and bawled curses at the top of his voice.

Charley told him to stop moving. He waited until Boss's arms were still, then eased ahead until he could reach the older man's collar. "When I yell, you jump," Charlie called. He got his boots firmly against rock and threw all his weight backward as Boss jumped.

He came up out of the hidden hole on his back, floundering and cursing until Charley could hoist him to his feet and hold him until Boss got his footing. Charley yelled in his ear. "Don't talk so damned much. Just concentrate on where you're going."

The hardest part was out in thc center of the roadway where cresting water was well above their knees, with enough force to make it possible for them to get past toward the opposite storefronts only by using their combined strength. Charley was feeling for the plankwalk with one foot when he thought that even if the storm stopped right now, within the next ten minutes, by morning it was not going to be possible to cross the roadway without something to hold to, like the rope Boss had mentioned back at the cafe.

They were soaked, their boots were half full of silt, and they were cold to the bone. When they found a bench bolted to the wall of a store, they sat on it looking back where they had just crossed, panting like a pair of dogs who'd been treeing cats.

Charley was tired. He reached under his poncho; the cigar was an unraveled, soggy mess. He lifted it out, looked mournfully at it, and tossed it out where raging water carried it from sight within seconds.

A man was walking toward them from the lower end of town, widening his stride between overhangs and shortening it while beneath them. He saw the pair of shiny black-caped figures on the bench and veered toward them. He was as gray as a badger with a startlingly droopy black dragoon moustache. In the gloom of the overhang it was impossible to tell much about him except that he was a cowman. He halted, showed worn teeth in a thin smile, and shook his head. "I watched you cross over here. A man could drown out there."

Charley looked up. "Right now," he said, "I'm havin' a real hard time agreeing with what I once heard a preacher say back in Sioux Falls: That the Lord don't send anything to us that isn't to our benefit an' salvation."

The cowman laughed, moved away from a leak in the overhang, and considered them. They looked ragged, unkempt, and demoralized. He offered a suggestion. "You can put up at the jailhouse if you can't afford the roominghouse, which is full anyway with two an' three men to a bed. They got empty cells up there and the roof don't leak."

Boss leaned to arise as he replied dryly. "The trouble with that, mister, is that gettin' out of that jailhouse would be a hell of a lot harder than gettin' into it." He stood up and nudged Charley.

The cowman watched them go trudging northward in the direction of Walt Barlow's place without even glancing at the warm lampglow on their left as they passed the jailhouse.

When they reached Barlow's gate, Charley spoke his thoughts. "We know who one of them was that attacked the camp, an' we know Baxter's going to be after us the minute the ground firms up enough to hold horses, and that leaves me wondering. With the law against us in Harmonville, with us being unable to leave, maybe we'd ought to do what an old soldier told me one time: Don't wait for trouble, because if you do you'll be too busy defending yourself to take charge of things, an' if you can't take charge you're going to lose."

Boss scowled with water coursing down his face. "What are you talking about?"

"The town marshal. Lock him up in his own jail until we can hitch up and get the hell away from here."

"You got water on the brain, Charley. He's got friends. You heard what he said about possemen here in town."

"Boss, while we've been doin' other things that son of a bitch has been sittin' down there in his jailhouse organizing folks against us, sure as hell. If we don't strike first he's going to nail our hides to his jailhouse wall."

This time Boss did not argue, but simply turned up toward the house, reached the porch with Charley a few paces behind, shed his poncho, and knocked on the door as he beat water from his hat.

Doctor Barlow appeared in the opening, backgrounded by warm lamplight. He looked them up and down, waved them inside, and looked them up and down again. They looked as if they'd been swimming in a mudhole. He said, "Come on out to the kitchen," and led the way. He tactfully ignored the tracks of mud they left.

His sister was not back there as he motioned them toward the popping cookstove. The kitchen was pleasantly warm and fragrant as Boss and Charley put their backs to the source of heat, unmindful of the steam that began to rise almost immediately from their soaked clothing. It had a unique aroma.

Doctor Barlow handed each of them a mug of hot coffee, then wagged his head. "You're getting to be well known in town," he told them. "I've heard several stories of your adventures crossing the road."

Boss was not interested. The heat on his back had a relaxing effect on his muscles, and the hot coffee did something similar under his hide. He said, "How's the boy, doctor?"

Barlow got himself a cup of coffee and stood by the kitchen table while he answered. "I have to tell you we were close to giving up on him last night." He drank coffee before continuing. Both the men by the stove had their eyes riveted to his face. Barlow smiled slightly. "Strange thing about fevers. I've seen people have them so bad they were hot to the touch, their lips dried and cracked, and they went out of their heads and were weak as kittens with sweat pouring out of them like rain."

Charley put his half-empty cup on the table. "That's real interesting. We don't give a damn about all those unfortunate folks, doctor. How is Button?"

Barlow's smile disappeared as he regarded Charley. At other times Waite had impressed him as a quiet, perhaps even a slightly diffident individual, but right now the look on Charley's face prompted Walt Barlow to make an adjustment of his earlier judgment. "The fever broke sometime after midnight," he said. "My sister heard the lad asking for water and fetched him some. He's still weak as a kitten but he's on the mend." Barlow took another sip of his coffee, still looking at Charley Waite. "He'll be too puny to be moved for a few days. Even if he wasn't, taking him down to your wagon in this weather might be the end of him; there'll be pneumonia going around. In his weakened condition . . . More coffee, gents?"

They politely declined. Even though steam was still rising from their soaked clothing, they felt warm and relaxed for the first time in several hours. No doubt the coffee contributed to that feeling. Boss approached the table, hauled out a chair to sit on, and asked if Button had made any more statements when he was out of his head. Doctor Barlow sat down too, shaking his head. "Not that I know of. But Sue's been closer to the lad than I have." He watched Charley come to the table before also saying, "It's been one thing after another, mostly old people. I've been in houses where there was a couple of inches of water covering the floor. I'm afraid when this is over there might be an epidemic."

He saw the look he was getting from Charley Waite and cleared his throat. "I don't know of any more statements he's made. I suppose you know who Butler is?"

Boss nodded woodenly. "One of Denton Baxter's men."

Barlow avoided their eyes and reached for his cup as he said, "Yes."

They waited for him to finish drinking. He saw the way they were gazing at him and pushed the cup aside, then leaned and clasped both hands atop the table. "Mister Baxter's a bad man to have for an enemy. He's got a lot of influence in the territory. The folks who aren't afraid of him, or who don't work for him in one capacity or another, don't like him."

Boss said, "You, doctor?"

"Well . . . I have reason not to like him. Not just for what he did to you men, but other things he's done to other people. He's a surly, overbearing, cold-blooded man." Doctor Barlow straightened up off the table and leaned back in his chair, looking from one of them to the other. Finally he said, "The surest way to lose your trade in my business is to buck whoever runs the countryside." He paused, continuing to look from one of them to the other, and said, "Stay away from your wagon tonight, gents."

Boss acted as though he had not heard. He arose in his drying clothes to refill his cup at the stove and return to his chair without looking at the medical man or speaking.

It was Charley who broke the silence. "It'll be Marshal Poole, because Baxter can't reach Harmonville."

Barlow nodded in silence. When someone entered from the roadway he jumped up and went toward the parlor. Boss looked at Charley Waite. "What was that you said while we were standin' out there gettin' drowned, about jumpin' him before he jumps us?"

Charley had no opportunity to repeat it; Sue Barlow entered the kitchen holding a soggy cape and bonnet. She smiled at them as her brother went after another cup of coffee. "Walt told you his fever broke," she said, taking a chair at the table and holding up a small gray bottle. "The apothecary made it up to strengthen Button's blood."

Charley took the little bottle, removed its cork and smelled it, then blinked and handed it back. "It ought to do that," he said dryly. The medicine had smelled to Charley as though it was at least seventy percent alcohol.

As her brother put a full coffee cup before her, he said Waite and Spearman were interested in whether Button had said anything that would interest them when he'd been out of his head, after mentioning the man named Butler.

She had to disappoint them. "He mumbled a little. If it was speech I couldn't understand it. Then last night the fever broke and this morning when I asked him who someone named Butler was, he didn't know. He had no recollection of hearing the name used at the wagoncamp."

Boss's thick brows climbed like caterpillars as he gazed at the handsome woman. "Well, now," he began, as he usually did when he did not understand something, "now, Miss Barlow, Button don't remember an' no one but you heard the name Butler. . . ."

She put a dead-level, gold-flecked tawny stare upon Boss Spearman. "He said it very distinctly. *Butler.* The rest of his raving was not as distinct, but that name was. That, and something about a one-armed man."

Charley took the initiative from Boss. "That's plenty good. We asked around town to find out who Butler is. I'm satisfied, Miss Barlow."

Later, almost dry and pleasantly revitalized by the coffee, they went out to the parlor where Sue Walton pointed to a closed door. "He's probably sleeping. It's late and he was worn out, or otherwise you could see him. I know he'd like that. He talks about you two as though you are a large part of his life. You and the man who was killed, Mister Harrison."

Her brother went over to the roadway door but did not open it. "They're waiting for you down at the wagon."

Boss regarded the doctor thoughtfully. "How many?"

Barlow did not know. "Marshal Poole and probably three or four of the men he uses as possemen and vigilantes." Barlow glanced at his sister, then back to Boss. "I've had to sew up people they overhauled. Quite a few over the years."

Charley had a question. "Just how much will Marshal Poole do for Baxter's interests?"

Sue answered. "Anything he has to do. There is a story around town that when Mister Baxter stampedes freegraze cattle, the owners are lucky if they recover half their animals. The other half go over the mountains to be sold, and Marshal Poole is paid to make sure no posse leaves town. They say Poole can be very persuasive when he wants to be, especially with the men he uses from time to time as possemen. Vigilantes, folks call them."

Her brother relinquished his grip on the doorknob. "We have a spare room off the kitchen. If you go down to your wagon there's a good chance you'll end up wrapped in blankets on the floor of the jailhouse storeroom."

Boss looked at his companion, and Charley stepped past Doctor Barlow to open the door. Neither of them said anything until they were on the porch, then they both thanked the Barlows for their hospitality and their help.

Chapter Twelve
More Mud But Less Water

Their ponchos were wet inside and clammy, but kitchen warmth as well as their partly dried clothing made them indifferent to this.

So did something else. The rain was no longer coming down in sheets, nor were the drops as large. The men halted beyond the Barlow picket fence to look upward. Nothing they could see up there indicated that the storm might be diminishing. Nevertheless, the rainfall lacked most of its furious intensity of an hour or two earlier. The squalling wind was weakening, and although the roadway more than ever resembled a wild river, the noise it made as it scoured Main Street down to bedrock was louder now than the rainfall.

Charley looked southward. There was not a soul in sight as far as he could see: no horses, wagons, or people. But there were occasional lighted windows. Understandably, merchants with perishable inventories were in their stores fighting the rising water to prevent it from flooding their buildings.

Boss faced his companion. Charley, who had been studying the farthest visible lights, said, "Is your handkerchief dry?"

Boss nodded.

Charley started down the awash plankwalk, stopped in a recessed doorway, and without saying a word, lifted out his six-gun, tugged the dry handkerchief from his rear pocket, and went to work unloading his six-gun and ridding it of silt. Boss did the same, but without being so quiet. "Instead of sneaking around in the dark trying to find them—if they're waiting to ambush us down there—it'd be better, an' a hell of a lot less chancey, if we just walked into the jailhouse and grabbed Poole."

Charley was wiping each individual bullet when he replied. "If he's alone, boss. And if he's in there." Charley hoisted up one side of his poncho, hooked it beneath his shell belt, holstered his weapon, and cocked an eye at Spearman. "Time to go around to the back alley," he said, and led off.

They sank to their ankles in mud the moment they left the duckboards to reach the alley through a littered space between two buildings. It made a man sweat just lifting one foot, then the other, each boot carrying forward more than a pound of mud.

The wind had died completely. The rainfall, although without its previous force, was still steady.

The alley was a quagmire. When Charley reached a rickety fence to lean on as he flung mud from his feet, he said, "If that back door isn't barred I'll eat your hat."

"Then what'n hell did we come around here for?"

"Because I don't like walkin' into a lighted room with maybe three or four enemies in it."

Boss had to be satisfied with what, to him, was not a complete answer, because Charley was moving in the direction of the jailhouse's rear wall. Boss shrugged and followed. When they were close to the rear door of the jailhouse, he tucked up his poncho on the right side and dried a wet palm on the protected part of his britches.

The door was not barred.

Charley opened it very carefully. Smoke scent and lamp glow came back toward the doorway. They stepped into a large storeroom, tiptoed ahead to another door, this one open, and looked into Marshal Poole's office.

It was empty.

Charley looked back and wagged his head. When they returned to the muddy alleyway Boss said, "What did you expect when you found the door unbarred? He left by the alleyway."

"Left for where, Boss?"

The larger, older man raised an arm from which the shiny black poncho hung suspended like a glistening wing, pointing southward.

They could not see down there for more than a dozen or so yards, and the monotonous drizzle of the rain drowned out whatever southward sounds there might have been.

Charley finally said, "We got to be right the first time, Boss, because sure as hell he isn't alone down there. They'll maybe have one man in the wagon, another one or two inside the livery barn down near the alley, and depending on how many there are, they might have another one or two hidden in other places."

Boss stood with rainwater trickling down from the front of his hat, peering southward. When he eventually spoke he was bitter. "My moneybox, Charley."

"Yeah. Right now I'm more worried about our hides. They'll be watching."

Boss continued to look southward. "Damned rain," he growled.

Charley's retort was offhand because he really was not thinking about the storm. "Yeah. But if it wasn't raining and if it was daylight, we'd never get near the wagon. . . . Boss, sure as hell they know every approach we can make: the roadway out front, this here alley, even the opposite side of Main Street where we'd come out if we used the alleyway over there to keep 'em from seein' us when we got down there."

When Boss said, "Yeah," Charley nudged him and began walking across the alley westward. Within town limits the ground was trampled and mushy. Out farther where rooted grass made walking a springy business without much sinking, they made good time.

Boss hiked along, humped slightly forward, in appearance for all the world in the shrouded, misty night like a large, perhaps prehistoric bird. He said nothing. Neither did Charley as he continued due west. Out where he finally stopped, though, he faced around and spoke. "If we angled right, we'd ought to be in line with the wagon across from the livery barn, but about a half mile west."

Boss understood finally, looked back, and let go a rattling breath. Walking that far, even on firm ground, was something he had not done in years. That's why God, or someone anyway, had given horses four legs and a small brain: so folks wouldn't have to walk.

Charley looked at his companion. Boss nodded, so Charley started back just as a biting little vagrant wind came knifing southward. It passed as swiftly as it had arrived, and while there was no more wind, it had pretty well chilled the ponchoed hikers before hastening southward. Boss said, "Has it come to you, Charley, that maybe Gawd don't like freegrazers neither?"

Up ahead the scattered lights from house windows were beginning to wink out. Evidently a lot of apprehensive townfolks had been listening to the diminishing rainfall and had finally decided to go to bed because the storm was either wearing itself out or was moving on. In either event the worst seemed to be over.

Something that had been noticeably lacking before, and which probably no one in Harmonville had been concerned about, occurred now: Several town dogs began barking. Boss plodded along, adding this to their other problems, but Charley was not that pessimistic. Dogs usually barked at night. Until recently they'd had little to bark at and most likely had been inside either houses or sheds to avoid the fury of the storm. With the storm abating they were once again out where they could pick up scents.

Charley ignored the dogs and concentrated on seeing the public corrals, their wagon, and a couple of sheds across the alley from the livery barn.

He saw the barn first. It had once been whitewashed. The rain had heightened what little color was left. By daylight the whitewash was barely noticeable. They were making a slow advance when the diminishing rainfall turned into a drizzle. Moments later, while the drizzle continued to come down, the low clouds began to be shredded by what must have been a high wind. The resulting moonlight helped visibility.

They continued toward the rear of the barn until they heard horses in a corral and stopped to listen. It may have been the end of the downpour as well as weak moonlight, which was a little better than no light at all, that had started the horses milling in their enclosure.

Boss reached to tap Charley's shoulder. He pointed a few degrees southward of the barn where someone just lit a sulfur match. The match flared briefly and sputtered. Charley had not thought they were as close as they were. Now he could see the silhouettes of two men lighting smokes very briefly before the match flared out.

Boss said, "They were in the barn."

Charley nodded. He had already made the same guess. They had been inside the barn near the alley opening to remain dry and had emerged when the moon arrived and the rain dwindled to a drizzle.

Now at least they knew where two of them were.

Charley removed his hat, pulled the poncho over his head, and dropped it. Wet ponchos reflected light.

Boss also shed his poncho as they began moving again, more slowly and cautiously now. Once Boss leaned over and whispered, "You figured right. They aren't watchin' open country west of town; they're watching the roadway an' the alley."

Charley's reply was curt. "Hope so. It's about time we had some luck."

They used the rear of an old shed to mask their approach. When they got up there and moved to the southern corner, they could see the wagon. In fact, they could have hit it with a rock. They could also see a yard or so into the livery barn. Farther in was pitch dark.

What they did not see was men, and they were what Charley sought. He wanted something better than a guess as to how many there were.

Boss whispered, "If we can get inside the shed it'll be dark an' we can take our time locating them."

Charley did not respond. The trick would be to slip down the side of the shed without being detected. He led off toward the opposite side, waited, watched and listened, then inched around and moved furtively with the water-darkened old dry wood as his background. What put his heart in his mouth was that damned moonlight.

Someone stamping through alleyway mud stopped Charley until he knew the man was south of the shed, not north. He led off again. They reached the corner, hesitated briefly, then whipped around, hugging wood all the way, and got inside the old shed.

There was a big untidy stack of firewood in there. The entire front of the shed was open, as was the case with most woodsheds. They were feeling their way to avoid rattling any wood, when a man's words were carried distinctly to them.

"They ain't up there. Doc only said they'd been there."

Another voice, this one reedy-high, asked how long ago that had been, and the original speaker answered shortly. "He didn't say. In fact, he wasn't real helpful at all."

The reedy-voiced man spoke again. "Well, if it was maybe an hour back an' they ain't showed up down here, why then they're maybe at the roominghouse—or somewhere else."

A third voice spoke, this one deep, resonant, and drawling. "You want us to search for them, marshal? They got to be in town."

There was a long delay before the original speaker replied. "You fellers stay here. They might try to sneak around to their wagon. I'll go look at the roominghouse and maybe a few other places. . . . Where's George?"

"In the wagon. Maybe asleep. You know George."

"Go see. Put a little scare into him so's he'll stay awake."

Charley eased down upon a round of fir firewood and shoved back his hat. When Boss sat down beside him he could see that Waite was smiling.

Boss whispered. "It might be easier goin' after the marshal than hangin' around here waiting to catch these fellers."

Charley absently nodded, seeming to acknowledge that he had heard what had been said, rather than because he liked Boss's suggestion.

He raised an arm in the darkness. One of the townsmen was raising each foot high, clear of the mud, before putting it down again. He was approaching the woodshed. The way he was doing it made him look like a stork. Being that careful of stepping into more mud was an exercise in futility; there was nothing but mud, not just in the alley but everywhere else.

Boss and Charley faded in opposite directions

with the tumbled mound of firewood to conceal their movements.

The oncoming man reached the front of the shed and came in a few feet where the higher interior was fairly dry, then turned his back to be able to watch the alley both north and south, and went to work rolling a cigarette.

Chapter Thirteen
Ragged Clouds

Boss was closest to the vigilante, whose tobacco smoke came lazily back into the shed. He had time to consider the situation, and while he was not entirely sure he could sneak up on the watcher from the rear, he was certain that whatever happened had to be accomplished in silence, or otherwise the other watchers would hear the commotion, drizzle or no drizzle.

Boss looked around in the gloom, saw a bone-dry old scantling that had been flung against the north wall of the shed, picked it up, and began his stalk.

The smoker flipped his quirley forward, where it fell into soft mud and winked out. The man stretched, reached inside his shirt to scratch, then twisted to find something to sit on. The fir rounds made an ideal improvised seat. He rolled a dry one close to the front overhang and sat down on it.

Boss paused between soundless strides seeking sign of Charley Waite. He was unsuccessful and worried for fear that Charley might also be stalking the seated man. This was not one of those situations that required two men.

Somewhere beyond Boss's vision southward a nightbird whistled. It was not a very good imitation. The seated man arose, stepped out almost to the end of the roof where drizzle would have soaked him, and peered to his right.

Fearful the man might turn completely around when he returned to his seat, Boss sank to one knee hoping to blend with the big pile of firewood.

But the stranger did not turn. He stepped fully forward into the drizzle and made his own poor imitation of a nightbird. Someone called guardedly from the direction of the campwagon, his voice quick and exultant. "Them bastards had money in here."

The man Boss was stalking turned quickly toward the wagon. "Money?"

"Yeah. I found a tinbox buried under a flour sack."

"How much money?"

"How in hell would I know? It's dark in here."

The vigilante was quiet, probably speculating about what he should do—abandon his post to go see the tinbox, or remain where he was?

Another voice, reedy and quick, spoke from the interior of the barn. "George?"

The man in the wagon answered shortly. "What?"

"Bring it in here."

"I'm not supposed to leave the wagon."

"George? To hell with the wagon. They've had plenty of time to get down here. They ain't coming. Bring the box in here and we'll divvy up."

That deep, drawling voice addressed the watcher up at the woodshed from somewhere southward of the barn in the alleyway. "Paul, you keep watch out here. George, do like Alf said, fetch the box into the barn. I don't think they're coming either. We been waitin' for more'n two hours. . . . George?"

"All right," replied the man in the wagon.

Boss waited for the man called Paul to return to his seat in the shed, but he did not do it. Evidently this abrupt and interesting development concerning Boss's money had made all the tiring watchers alert again.

The drizzle was slackening; more torn and ragged clouds allowed more light to reach earth. Paul moved back where drizzle could not reach him but he did not go all the way back to the pile of wood. Boss had to resume his stalk toward a clear area of perhaps six or seven feet between the rounds and the man named Paul.

If the watcher heard anything, or even if he just casually turned, he was going to see Boss when he stepped into the clear area.

Boss abandoned the scantling and brushed a hand over the handle of his holstered Colt, shortened his stride, and concentrated on making no sound as he headed toward the front of the shed six inches at a time, scarcely breathing and not once taking his eyes off the watcher's back.

The man craned to watch a shadow flicker through mist from the wagon toward the dark opening of the livery barn, then wagged his head, rummaged for his tobacco sack, and stood hip-shot as he went to work rolling a smoke.

Boss would be in plain sight now if Paul turned. Paul pocketed the little Durham sack and looked down as he completed the roll, then raised the quirley to lick the fold before pinching the end to be lighted. Boss waited until Paul's hands were up near his face before drawing his Colt and cocking it.

That unmistakable sound did not carry beyond Paul, who seemed suddenly to have turned to stone, still holding the cigarette up near his face.

Boss spoke in a strong whisper. "Just face around an' keep your hands up where they are."

Paul turned. His features looked unhealthily gray inside the shed. His eyes found Boss without difficulty and did not move.

From Paul's left side Charley Waite appeared like a ghost to lift out the watcher's six-gun and toss it beyond the wood pile. Charley gave Paul a light shove toward the interior of the shed while Boss kept his eyes on their prisoner without lowering the dog of his six-gun.

Paul was a man of average height with a look of dissipation, but that could have been caused by the poor light and the grayness of the hour. He was probably in his forties. When Charley went over him for hideouts and found none, Paul finally found his voice.

"You're not goin' to make it. The marshal's been passing word around that you're freegrazers."

Boss said, "What were you doing out at our wagoncamp a few nights back?"

Paul's bafflement was obviously genuine when he replied. "What the hell are you talkin' about?

I never heard of any of you fellers until you brought that boy to town."

Boss shrugged. It had been a shot in the dark. He had not really thought these townsmen had been part of the group that had killed Mose.

"How many others are around here?" he asked, and Paul did not even hesitate. In fact, he sounded vindictively exultant. "More'n you two can handle. Three, not counting the marshal."

Boss smiled without a shred of humor. "The marshal's lookin' for us around town. Get belly down and don't make a damned sound or I'll bust your skull like a pumpkin."

Paul got flat out amid the sawdust, pieces of bark, and ancient dust. Charley tied his arms behind his back, lashed his legs at the ankle, and as added insurance, gagged him with his own neckerchief.

They left him lying there, went forward to the front of the shed, did not notice that there were now only a few veiny runnels of rainwater coursing in the mud, considered the opposite barn opening, the approaches to it, saw no one, heard nothing, and walked out into plain sight to cross toward the faded, whitewashed rear wall of the livery barn.

Charley was encouraged; he was sure the men inside the barn were busily divvying up Boss's money. Boss, on the other hand, did not think beyond the fact that he was being robbed of his operating capital. Where he halted beside Charley with his back brushing whitewashed rough siding, he leaned to whisper something, but Charley's abruptly raised left hand stopped him from making a sound.

Somewhere, a man was approaching. Charley

had picked up the sound of boots slogging through clinging mud. The sound appeared to be coming from either inside the barn or outside it southward. He was troubled by his inability to pinpoint the origin of the noise, but was perfectly satisfied as to what was making it.

He twisted to whisper to Boss, and froze.

Behind them at the corner of the building a man was standing in watery moonlight holding a six-gun. It had not occurred to Charley that those footsteps might be approaching from the north.

The shadow with the gun was partly obscured by the barn's square shadow, partly by the poor light, and partly by his attire, which was dark. The man did not raise his voice. "Drop the guns."

Boss, startled to hear someone behind, swung his head before Charley said, "Easy, Boss. It's the marshal. He's got a six-gun aimed at your back."

Charley lifted out his weapon, looked unhappily at the mud, and let the weapon drop. It did not make a sound as it sank.

Boss did the same.

Marshal Poole gestured with his weapon at the same time he raised his voice to alert the men in the barn. "I got 'em. They're comin' into the barn." In a quieter tone as he wigwagged with his Colt, he ordered Boss and Charley to start walking.

The moonlight, which reached a yard or so inside the barn from the alley, did not make even a dent in the darkness farther in. When Waite and Spearman walked in with Marshal Poole driving them, there was not a soul in sight, just a dented old tinbox with a smashed hasp over against a stall front where it had been tossed after being emptied.

A reedy voice called to the lawman, "Damned if you didn't." Three men appeared from different areas, guns in hand, to stop a few feet away and stare. One of the men grinned and said in a deep, slow voice, "Were they at the roominghouse?"

Poole's retort was curt. "No. They was stalking you from out back. George, if you'd been in the damned wagon you'd have seen them. What the hell are you doing in here, all three of you?"

It became clear that the three watchers had made a pact, after dividing Boss's money among them, not to say a word about it to Marshal Poole. George sounded a little whiney when he said, "The damned tarp leaked. Besides, we was about to give up. We been getting rained on and all since—"

Poole broke in fiercely. "Where'd that box come from? It wasn't in here before."

Boss answered flintily. "It come out of our wagon. I kept my operatin' money in it. You want to know the rest, marshal? They was hollerin' back and forth out there makin' enough noise to raise the dead after they found my box. They agreed to come in here and divvy up my money amongst them."

Marshal Poole's faintly seen face formed a slow scowl. "Where's Paul?"

One of his vigilantes replied quickly. "Across the alley. He was to keep watch while we was in here. Over at the woodshed."

Poole stared at the speaker. "Then why didn't he see me an' hear me when I come up behind these two?"

There was no response.

The marshal pointed his pistol barrel toward

the broken tinbox. "Pick it up, George. Each of you put the money back into it you taken out of it."

They obeyed sullenly and the man with the deep voice said, "Al, we been soaked, half froze, hungry, bored stiff, and worn out from standin' around here half the damned night. Besides that, there wasn't much money in the damned box . . . A hunnert dollars. Split three ways that don't hardly even make wages."

Marshal Poole holstered his gun, ignoring his companions, and gazed at his captives. Without a word he gestured for them to walk toward the front of the barn and the main thoroughfare. His three men started to follow, but one called ahead, "I'll tell Paul where we're going. Up to the jailhouse." As this man hurried back in the direction of the alley, Boss and Charley exchanged a look.

The sky was clearing, the moon was descending, and although the roadway was still a millrace, there was no longer a flooding crest out in the center of it, and for most of the walk to the jailhouse it was possible to see the plankwalk underfoot.

When they got up there Marshal Poole herded his prisoners in first, and he was followed by two of his vigilantes. The men were seeking places to sit when the third vigilante burst in helping another man whose circulation was not very good. The third man glared accusingly at the prisoners but addressed Marshal Poole. "They left him tied in the woodshed across from the barn."

Poole was not sympathetic. He considered the man named Paul, who sat on a wall bench and rubbed his arms as he looked back. Eventually Poole said, "All right," and tossed the tinbox to them. "Divide it an' go on home. I'll see you in the morning."

After they had left, the lawman told his prisoners not to move off their benches while he stoked up the stove and put the coffeepot on. They watched Poole work without moving.

When he returned to his table he perched on a corner of it regarding Boss and Charley and began wagging his head. "You should have left the country like Mister Baxter told you to do."

Boss eyed the lawman sulfurously, but remained silent.

Marshal Poole shifted from the corner of the table to his chair behind it. "A storm like this one was . . . I doubt like hell if you'll find any of your cattle."

Neither of his prisoners looked away or opened his mouth. Poole leaned, clasped both hands atop the table, and gazed at them. "I got a whole slew of charges against you, from disturbing the peace to committing public nuisances. And those are only for openers." Marshal Poole went to test the coffee, filled a cup for himself, and returned to his desk with it. "When Mister Baxter gets back down here he'll push the other complaints. Like attackin' his riders, tryin' to kill them, running damned freegraze cattle over his grassland. Y'know, when the judge gets to Harmonville maybe next month, you boys will be lucky to see the outside of prison walls for ten years.

"On your feet. Past that cellroom door and be real careful."

Chapter Fourteen
Sunshine

Charley awakened first. Boss was lying on his back across the cell, one leg draped over the edge of his bunk, snoring with sufficient resonance to create echoes.

Charley considered his boots, left them lying, and walked over to the strap-steel cell door to look around.

There were no other prisoners. There were six cells along a stone corridor, three to a side. The place smelled of mold and dampness. But what caught and held Waite's attention was dazzlingly brilliant sunlight coming through a high, narrow, barred window in the opposite cell's front wall. He sighed, listened to the sounds of human activity out in the roadway, and turned as Boss coughed, opened his eyes, and drifted sleep-fuzzy eyes in Charley's direction.

When Charley said, "Good morning," Boss

grunted up onto one elbow, saw the sunshine, and got heavily to his feet. He gazed at his soggy boots and said, "Only an idiot would say good morning."

A half hour later the marshal brought two tin plates of something that seemed to be a cross between stew and hash, shoved the plates under the door, and considered his prisoners. "You two look like somethin' a cat would drag in."

They ignored him, got their plates, and sat on the edge of their bunks to eat. When Boss had scraped up the last of whatever he had eaten, he cocked an eye at Charley. Marshal Poole went back up front, slammed the cellroom door, and Boss said, "End of the trail."

Charley was holding a soggy Durham sack and gazing at it when he replied. "Naw. It's not over until they blow the bugle."

He arose and moved to the front of the cell again. The scent of mold lingered, but the cellroom was warming up. Those men out in the roadway were calling back and forth. Charley thought he heard scrapers and wagons out there. He could imagine how much dumping, spreading, and hauling it was going to take to make Main Street usable again.

Boss spoke from his bunk. "I don't think that getting out of here would do much good. Like the marshal said last night, the cattle will be scattered to hell and gone."

Charley turned to study Spearman's haggard countenance. "I wasn't thinkin' about the cattle," he told Boss. "I was thinkin' about what happened to Mose and Button. I'd like to be out of here before Baxter rides in."

Boss said, "How?"

Charley did not reply but went back to place his soggy boots where the slanting sunshine would reach them, then sat on the edge of the bunk again. "I don't know how. I got a bad feelin' about the future, Boss."

"I already told you, it's the end of the trail. Charley, freegrazing ain't like it used to be. Sure, we wasn't popular but, hell, it never before came to anything like this." Boss was silent for a moment before speaking again. "Baxter," he muttered without adding anything, and arose to pace the cell. "I'm too old to start over, Charley."

"If Poole and Baxter have their way, Boss, we'll both start over, maybe down in Yuma prison. I've heard some bad stories about that place." As he said this, Charley arose to move over into the sunshine. "I'd like to know how Button is."

Marshal Poole returned later in the day to put drinking water in their cells and to hand each of them an oversized coffee can. As he was relocking the door he said, "The judge'll be here sooner than I thought. From what the stage driver said, the storm didn't cause as much damage up north as it did down here." Poole leaned to look in at them. "I met Sue Barlow in the road a while back an' told her I had you two in here an' she said she'd be along directly to see you." Poole's slatey eyes were fixed on Charley. "She's foolish takin' up for you two. Her an' her brother both."

Boss ignored most of all this to ask about Button, but evidently Sue had said nothing about the kid to Marshal Poole, because all he offered was a frown before he departed.

Charley spread his tobacco in sunlight too, very carefully, along with his wheatstraw cigarette papers. Boss watched this with something close to indifferent interest. He said, "I was thinkin' about getting out of the damned cattle business anyway. But my idea was to sell off the cattle to have enough money to start up in somethin' else. Like maybe a saloon somewhere. Built up off the ground, with a roof that don't leak and a big stove. A man could stay warm an' dry in winter and cool in summer."

Charley looked surprised. "You never mentioned this before," he said, returning to the edge of his bunk.

Boss did not look up when he replied. "But I been thinkin' about it. It's not just being a free-grazer an' having just about everyone dislikin' me, it's spendin' about half the year in mud or frost, or maybe blisterin' sun. Charley, if it's not a deluge it's a drought. I'm gettin' too old for it anymore."

Waite leaned back until his shoulders were against the wall, studying his companion. If Boss sold out and quit, Charley would have to strike out again. Maybe take Button along. He'd worked for other outfits, but not for a while, and he'd been comfortable with Boss Spearman.

As the afternoon wore along, the noise in the roadway increased rather than diminished. Charley was finally able to roll a smoke. Boss was napping when the marshal returned to the cellroom with Sue Barlow. She was shocked at their appearance. Before when she'd seen them they had been muddy, soaked, rumpled, and disreputable looking, but not so slack and demoralized as this. She ignored the lawman when she said, "Button is on the mend. He's even beginning to eat."

Charley nodded at her. Boss was sound asleep, on his side this time so he did not snore.

She paused a long time before speaking again. "I asked if we could post bail for you, Mister Waite. The marshal said no."

Charley finally pushed forward to the edge of the bunk again. "Surc good to see sunshine again, ain't it?"

She nodded woodenly, then turned without another word. Marshal Poole threw Charley a triumphant smile before passing from sight following Sue Barlow up front.

She was white to the hairline as she faced Poole. "Can't they at least wash? They look awful. Like trapped animals."

The lawman sat down at his table looking up at her. "They don't leave that cell until the circuit-riding judge gets here to try them."

She returned his steady stare for a moment, then walked to the door and out into the noisy roadway without speaking or looking back. When she got home, Button was at the kitchen table with her brother. She sank into a chair and told them what she had seen and what she had been told. Button's appetite dwindled to nothing as he listened. Doctor Barlow was gazing into an empty coffee cup, and neither looked at her nor opened his mouth.

She spoke sharply. "Walt! He's going to railroad them and you know it. Otherwise, he'll hold them until Mister Baxter rides to town, and that could be even worse for them. You know that too."

Her brother leaned back in his chair, eyes raised to her face. "I'm a doctor, Sue, not a gunfighter. Even if I was, Al Poole's vigilantes add up to more guns than a sane man could even think about facing."

She said, "There was to be someone, Walt. Something we can do."

He shook his head at her. "If they weren't free-grazers, maybe. Just maybe."

She stood up, ignoring Button's stricken look as she said, "All right. You set bones and dose folks for fevers," and flung out of the kitchen leaving her brother and Button staring after her. Neither of them moved until they heard the front door slam, then Button stood up. Doctor Barlow said, "Sit down, son, and finish your meal."

Button sat down but ignored the food to put a troubled look upon Doctor Barlow, who tried to be reassuring when he said, "I'll see what can be done."

Button was not very reassured. He left the kitchen for the room he had been staying in. He did not have time to close his door before a commotion out on the porch brought him back toward the parlor.

Across the parlor Doctor Barlow was scowling in the doorway of his examination room when the door burst open. Sue backed into the parlor gesturing for a large, burly man in a plaid shirt to head for the examination room. The big man was cradling a forlorn-looking dog in his arms. Behind him was a girl of about eleven or twelve, red-eyed and obviously desolated.

Walt stepped aside. The big man gently put the dog on Walt's examination table and turned a little apologetically. "I know you doctor people, not animals, but there's no one else. We tried the apothecary an' he sent us up here."

Walt approached the dog and winced. He had

obviously tangled with a skunk. The big man leaned to lift a foreleg and expose a bloody long gash to the bone. Walt told his sister to get a tourniquet, then raised the leg to exert pressure until most of the bleeding stopped. The little girl stood in ashen agony watching as Sue got the binder in place and gently turned it until there was no bleeding.

Walt used a razor to cut away the hair, cleansed the injury with carbolic acid, leaned as close as he could to estimate the amount of damage, then told the big man to hold the tourniquet and sent Sue for chloroform. The moment the dog went limp, Walt went to work.

Behind the girl, Button was standing in the doorway. She turned away, fighting back the tears. Button put a hand lightly on her shoulder and smiled. "She'll be all right."

"It's not a she, it's a he."

Button offered the little girl a handkerchief. She fiercely blew her nose and handed the handkerchief back. The older people did not seem to know they were back by the doorway.

When Walt was satisfied he was in control, he did not raise his head as he asked the big man what had happened.

"Tangled with a skunk who came out from under one of our wagons. I guess it was the only dry place the skunk could find. My daughter's dog picked up the scent."

Walt dryly said, "I can't imagine how he did that."

The big man went on though there had been no interpretation. "The dog couldn't really do much hunched down beneath the wagon, but he made a rush an' that skunk raked him down the inside of the leg with one paw."

"What happened to the skunk?" Walt asked, and got a quizzical look from the large man. "He got shot to death."

"The reason I asked," stated Walt, drawing open flesh together before each stitch, "is that if the skunk had hydrophobia, your dog may get it. If he gets it and bites anyone, they'll get it. There's no cure."

The large man answered solemnly. "Yeah, I know. I lost a good mule to the hydrophobia once. Bit by a crazy-mad coyote. That skunk didn't act crazy, just scairt and fighting mad."

Walt let the topic die and finished the sewing before stepping away so his sister could start the bandaging. He saw the girl and Button and smiled. "He'll be fine. Unless that was an infected skunk. It probably wasn't, but you keep watch on him, young lady. Don't let him get near you if he starts snarling or dripping saliva."

The large man dug in a faded trouser pocket and produced several silver cartwheels. Walt selected one. As the big man was returning the other coins to his pocket he said, "That's the dog's second close call. He got swept into the roadway in that storm. I tried to grab him but the current was too swift. Two stockmen was wading across. One of them caught the pup as he was whirling past and brought him to the plankwalk with him."

Button, Sue, and Walt stared at the man. Walt said, "Was one a big older man, the other one a husky, younger and shorter man?"

The girl's father nodded. "Yeah. I saw them at the cafe later. My brothers was in there havin' somethin' to eat before we went back to our wagoncamp on some high ground northeast of Harmonville. One big old man an' a shorter, stocky feller who was younger. You know them?"

Sue answered ahead of her brother. "Yes. The large older man is Boss Spearman. The other man is Charley Waite."

The large man smiled. "My little girl an' I owe them, ma'am. Do they live in town?"

Doctor Barlow replied dryly, "Down at the jailhouse."

The big man's eyes widened. "Prisoners? What'd they do?"

Button spoke from the doorway. "They're freegrazers. I'm one of them. A cowman told us to get out of the country, then killed Mose, tried to kill me, and—"

Sue interrupted. "Button, take the young lady to the kitchen and see if she'd like some of that apple pie under the saucepan."

Until they were gone not a word was said. Afterward, Sue explained everything to the large man, who went to a small chair and sat down as he listened. On the examination-room table the loudest sound after Sue had finished was the raspy breathing of the unconscious dog.

The big man drifted his gaze from Sue to her brother. Walt nodded. "It's the truth."

"An' the town marshal's some kind of partner to this cowman named Baxter?"

"Yes."

"An' that's why he's been after those freegrazers?"

"Yes."

The large man arose. "Those freegrazers didn't

kill anyone or steal horses or something else, did they?"

Sue vehemently shook her head.

The big man stood in thought for a moment before making a grunting sound as he cleared his throat before speaking. "I owe that big old man. My little girl would have lost her dog. She sets a world of store by that dog, an' I got to admit he's mannerly and friendly and all. Good around horses and mules. I'm a freighter. Me an' my two brothers. Doctor, anyone who does a good turn for my little girl does one for me, an' I'm a man who believes in repayin' a debt. A good debt or a bad debt."

The big man brushed past Walt to lift the inert dog in powerful arms. He went to the parlor and called loudly, "Annie? Time to go. Annie?"

She came with pie crumbs still on her face. The big man grinned. "Wipe your chin, Annie. Tell these folks thanks."

The little girl did better. She thanked them, then she curtsied. Sue bent over and kissed her, held her hand as they walked out to the porch, and stood watching until the large man and the small girl were out of sight.

Chapter Fifteen
Another Week

Three days after the ruined roadway had been graded back into shape, the morning coach from up north arrived in Harmonville with three passengers. Two were grizzled livestock buyers, both attired in riding coats that reached lower than their knees. Those two passengers headed straight for the saloon.

The third passenger was a rumpled man in a rusty dark suit, scuffed black boots, and an unbrushed dark hat who was wearing a string tie. He chewed cigars instead of regular chewing tobacco, had a close-cropped salt-and-pepper beard and a paunch that hung over his belt buckle. His name was Ambrose Collins. He was a circuit-riding territorial judge whose area included the eastern part of what would one day be the state of Arizona, and all the lower, or southern section of New Mexico.

His reputation matched the granite set of his jaw as well as the uncompromizing testiness of his gaze. When he entered Marshal Poole's office the lawman was frowning over a badly scrawled handwritten note a rough-looking rangeman had given him a few minutes earlier. The rangeman was sprawling in a chair holding a cup of coffee when Judge Collins walked in.

Marshal Poole looked up, still scowling. His features cleared in an instant. He arose and pushed out his hand. "Glad to see you, judge. Didn't expect you for another week or so."

Ambrose Collins shook hands and eyed the cowboy, whose curiosity had been piqued by the use of Collins's title. They nodded to each other, like circling dogs. Al Poole went after a cup of coffee for His Honor and squared around an old chair facing his desk.

He glanced at the cowboy. "All right. You can tell Mister Baxter I got the note."

The lanky man arose, put his cup aside, and said, "What'll I tell him?"

Marshal Poole reddened. "Just what I said, that I got his note."

The rider persisted. "He'll want to know what you are goin' to do."

Marshal Poole's eyes smouldered. "All you got to worry about is that you delivered the note." He and the rangeman exchanged a long look before the cowboy shrugged and went to the door. After he was gone Marshal Poole sat behind his desk to ask how the coach ride down to Harmonville had been.

Judge Collins's thick bony forehead protruded above sunk-set unsmiling eyes. He sipped coffee and studied the marshal. Eventually he said,

"Bumpy, wet. . . . Looks like you folks got the full brunt of it."

Poole briskly nodded. "We did. Like I never saw it rain before. There was chuckholes in the road you could bury a man in."

Ambrose Collins's eyes were fixed on the lawman's face like the eyes of a ferret. "You got trouble?" he asked, gesturing with his half-empty cup in the direction of the roadside door.

Poole spread both hands palms down. "Him? He's a rider for a stockman up near the foothills. Naw, it's not trouble." He smiled again. "I got two prisoners. When d'you want to hold court?"

Judge Collins drained his coffee and arose before replying. "In the morning. I been riding coaches since day before yesterday an' feel like I been yanked through a knothole. Is the roominghouse still in business?"

Poole nodded and watched the rumpled, heavy, older man leave his office. Then the marshal sank back in his chair, scowling in the direction of the cellroom door. Baxter's note had been short. He had completed a three-day roundup of those freegrazers' cattle and was getting ready to send them over the mountains with his riders. He and the two men he'd kept back would be coming down to Harmonville to take care of those prisoners he'd heard Poole had locked in his jailhouse. He expected to reach town by midafternoon. His suggestion was that Marshal Poole be out of town, a long way out of town, and remain away until after nightfall.

Poole dumped on his hat and strode diagonally across the repaired roadway to the saloon. It was midmorning, so the place was not crowded, but there were three freighters lined up at the bar like crows on a tree limb, saying very little as they considered their little whiskey glasses. When Marshal Poole entered, they studied him with bold eyes and said even less.

The barman approached Poole with raised eyebrows. He had served the town marshal for a long time, but never before in the middle of the morning. He set up a bottle and glass, hesitated long enough to realize that Poole was not in a talkative frame of mind, and went back up midway between the solemn freighters and the lawman, where his pail of greasy water was, and began fishing out glasses, which he dried on a limp old gray towel.

The saloon was quiet, but noise from the repaired roadway was loud and fairly regular. People who had been unable to move around much during the storm were making up for it now. Down at the emporium the place was full of women shoppers. Even the blacksmith's shop at the lower end of town opposite the livery barn and the public corrals was busy. Two men down there shaping and fitting hot shoes over anvils sent a familiar sound all over town.

One of Marshal Poole's vigilantes walked in out of what was shaping up to be a muggily hot day, settled beside the lawman, nodded for a glass, and softly said, "There's a circuit-ridin' judge in town."

Poole's scowl deepened. "I know that," he snapped.

The vigilante had the kind of reedy voice that carried even though he tried to keep it very low, particularly in the saloon, where there was no other sound.

The vigilante considered Poole's profile, downed his whiskey, and slouched in thought regarding the half-empty bottle. Eventually he straightened up as though to turn and depart as he said, "Marshal, there's a right nice pair of big horses go with that freegraze wagon." He paused to assess the effect this might have had, then continued. "We was wondering . . . countin' the wagon, which ain't worth much, and them big horses, we could get our wages by sellin' 'em."

Poole turned slowly. "Baxter's coming," he said, speaking so quietly his words would not carry beyond the other man. "He'll be here this afternoon."

"What of it, marshal?"

Poole's color darkened. "What of it! That damned judge is here, that's what of it! Dent Baxter is comin' to settle with the freegrazers for injurin' a couple of his men, and for grazing off his feed west of town."

The vigilante gazed at his companion. "You mean . . . ?"

Poole did not reply. He turned to reach for the bottle and refilled both their glasses. He dropped the second shot as straight down as he had dropped the first one. He blew out a fiery breath and said, "Either someone's got to ride north, find Baxter, and tell him about the judge bein' here an' for him not to come to town, or someone's got to get that damned judge out of town overnight."

The vigilante was still calmly regarding the agitated lawman. He did not touch his refilled glass. "How?" he asked softly.

Poole's retort was curt. "That's what I been trying to figure out since I came in here."

The vigilante glanced at the back-bar mirror, back to Marshal Poole, and then asked a question. "About them big horses and the wagon, marshal?

Paul, George, an' Buff is down at the poolhall. We saw you come up here. They're waitin'."

A vein near the lawman's temple seemed to swell as his face reddened. He clutched the little whiskey glass until his knuckles were white, but when he spoke his voice was very low. "You tell them that none of you goes near those horses nor that wagon. You understand? You don't do a damned thing until the judge leaves town. . . . Alf?"

"What?"

"Saddle up and ride north until you find Dent Baxter and tell him to stay out of town until the damned judge leaves."

"It's a long ride, marshal."

Poole rammed a fist into his trouser pocket, drew forth a silver cartwheel, and slammed it down atop the bar so hard the barman's head snapped up and those more distant freighters who were still nursing their jolt glasses turned to stare.

"Go!" snarled the lawman.

Alf picked up the silver dollar and walked briskly out of the saloon.

The marshal was ready to leave also when three old men shuffled in and the barman sighed, gave his head a slight wag, and as the old gaffers headed for a round table near the woodstove, he drew off three nickel glasses of beer, picked up a box of wooden matches and a deck of greasy old playing cards and went over to the table where the gaffers were shedding disreputable old coats and getting settled for their game of matchstick poker. They paid the barman. He went back behind his bar, saw one of the freighters eyeing him pensively, and leaned to say, "Every damned day, rain or shine—except durin' the storm," and went on down to finish drying oily shot glasses.

As Al Poole was crossing toward the roadway doors, one of the old gaffers casually hailed him. "Marshal, there's a feller waitin' for you at the jailhouse. I seen him walk in a few minutes ago."

"Fat feller dressed all in black?"

"Naw. Big old rawboned man, maybe a little older'n you."

Poole walked out into the damp heat, struck out for the opposite plankwalk, and turned southward.

Behind him three men emerged from the saloon and stood watching the lawman's progress. One of them said, "I'll take care of the gent with the squeaky voice," and turned southward. The other two lingered long enough to share a plug and get their cuds settled properly, then ambled diagonally in the direction of the poolhall, which was between the abstract office and the harness shop.

There was considerable roadway traffic, mostly pedestrian and mostly female, but there were a few horsemen and a couple of rigs sinking into the roadway fill.

Doctor Barlow was across the road, heading briskly in the direction of the roominghouse, from which an agitated proprietor had come breathlessly to summon him for an ill man. The roominghouse owner had already diagnosed the sick man and had told Barlow it was the flux, which was bad enough, but when his other guests had heard what had put the ill man down, they vacated the place; some had left so hurriedly that they'd neglected to pay up.

Walt Barlow saw Marshal Poole enter the jailhouse. So did a number of other townsmen. They paid no heed, but if they could have seen Poole's face as he went to sit at his desk while his visitor was speaking to him, they would have been quite interested.

The rangy older man was sitting with his hat shoved back, long legs thrust out, thumbs hooked in a heavy old shell belt. He had not introduced himself when the marshal had walked in and nodded, but had simply said, "It's a right lively town, marshal. I been in a lot just like it, but this is the first time I been marooned in a strange place 'cause of rain." The older man was gazing at his boot toes as he spoke. "It wasn't my choice, an' for a fact I wasn't real sure I would ever leave Harmonville the way that water built up. . . . Can you swim, marshal?"

Poole had his fingers interlocked in front of him atop the table. He shook his head while eyeing his visitor in silence. The man made him uncomfortable.

"Neither can I, marshal. I can do a lot of things, but I never learned to swim, an' from my upstairs window at the roominghouse, I never saw so damned much water out of a riverbed in my life." The stranger raised flinty blue eyes. "By the way, they got a sick man down there. He's got the bloody flux. You know how that can spread, marshal. I can tell you from experience, it can put a whole town flat on its back."

Al Poole finally unclasped his hands and leaned back. "We got a doctor. He'll take care of it. Now then, I got a lot to do this morning, so . . ."

The flinty blue eyes remained calmly on Al Poole as the stranger said, "Sure. I understand. Your town's been through a real calamity.

There'll be plenty for a lawman to do. My name's Dallas Pierce. I was on a coach the day when that roadway out there was runnin' water better'n knee high. A man couldn't see nothin' but water. There was two fellers crossin' over when we come down toward the corralyard. One of 'em, a stocky feller, hurled himself at the nearside leader and forced the horses to turn right or they'd have stepped into a hole deep enough to hide a big calf in. That damned horse swerved, the driver was cussin' something fierce. As the coach swung clear of the hole . . . I'm here to tell you if one front wheel had gone into that hole, marshal, the rig would have gone over. As the coach swung clear and brushed past that stocky feller, him and I was no more'n twelve inches apart an' face to face. He didn't just save the horses an' the coach. He saved us passengers who was inside. Sure as hell if that stage had gone over, we'd have been bad hurt if we didn't drown."

Marshal Poole continued to eye Dallas Pierce as he slowly leaned forward on the tabletop again. "Dallas Pierce?"

"Yes." The rangy man's eyes were stone-steady as he replied, without adding anything to that one word.

"Dallas Pierce, the U.S. marshal?"

This time the rawboned older man simply nodded his head.

Al Poole was silent for a long while, studying his visitor. Finally he said, "The road's fixed now. The stages are running again."

Dallas Pierce returned to the study of his boot toes. "I was goin' to leave yesterday an' missed the damned evening stage. This morning I was standin' out front of the cafe when the southbound rolled in." Pierce's gaze came up. "You know who was on it?"

Poole was beginning to have an upset stomach. "Yeah. Judge Collins."

Dallas Pierce shot up to his feet. He gazed at Al Poole with a faint smile. "Ambrose Collins. I've known that old high-binder for fifteen years. I figured I'd stay over for a day or two, let him buy me a few drinks. . . . Marshal?"

"Yes."

"I was over in the corralyard earlier seein' about some schedules, and one of the yardmen told me you had that feller who maybe saved my life, and sure as hell saved them horses and the old coach, in one of your cells. Him and the other feller, the big older man."

Poole arose slowly. "They are freegrazers. They attacked some rangemen in the night, hurt one real bad. They been grazing off grass that belongs to one of our biggest cowmen."

Dallas Pierce nodded thoughtfully, turned, and left the jailhouse without another word.

Chapter Sixteen
Dealing a New Hand

The man who managed the poolhall for its owner, who was the same man who owned the saloon across the road, was named Hugh Fenwick. He'd been suffering from a bad back since a horse had fallen with him eight years earlier.

Hugh was gray and a little pinched in the face. At one time he had not only been a good stockman but had earned quite a reputation as a horse breaker.

Now he was sitting erectly on the special chair the town carpenter had built for him while three local men he knew were playing pool at one of his tables and three other men he did not know but had seen around town lately were racking up at the other table.

Hugh picked up a ragged newspaper. In a place like Harmonville it did not matter whether news was fresh or not because it would have no local effect.

His patrons were joking a little, among themselves and not with the players at the other table. Outside, Doctor Barlow walked northward in the direction of his cottage. On the opposite side of the roadway a man called and waved. Barlow waved back.

A large blue-tailed fly came into the poolhall. The manager watched it circling for a while, then carefully folded his newspaper. But the fly moved toward the distant tables, so the manager unfolded his paper. He was speculating about the advantages of a back brace advertised in the newspaper, which looked exactly like a lady's corset, when someone said, "Mister, that's the third time. The next time you punch me with your damned elbow I'm going to pull it off you."

The manager did not have a chance to get off his chair before the brawl erupted. He bellowed at the top of his voice. The effect was the same as though he'd said nothing. He leaned to support himself with both hands on a little table as he eased out of the chair.

One of the strangers had slow-witted big George Kendal maneuvered into a corner, and while George was as strong as an ox, so long as he was unable to get out of the corner he was unable to make much of an impression on the man facing him. His adversary was standing wide-legged and flat down. While George was being peppered by stinging blows, the stranger was ducking and weaving. George lunged at him, swinging like a windmill, but the lighter man hit him in the middle, which folded him over, then hit him alongside the head, and George went down without a sound.

Across the room, beyond the farthest pool table, drawling, big, deep-voiced Buff Brady was slugging it out toe-to-toe with another of the strangers. The manager with the bad back got to his wall rack and was standing there holding a heavy pool cue. It wasn't pain that kept him over there, but simply fascination.

Buff Brady had a reputation in Harmonville for being able to absorb more punishment and give back more of the same than anyone around. Unlike slow-witted big George Kendal, Brady was neither dense nor clumsy. What held the poolhall manager stone-still was the way neither Buff nor the man facing him was yielding a step. He grounded the cue and leaned on it.

The third stranger was down on the floor with Paul Sawyer, but Paul's heart was not in it. He'd been having trouble with his arms and legs since his circulation was cut off by tight bindings in the woodshed across the alley from the livery barn.

That fight ended with Paul saying, "That's enough," and covering his face until his adversary stood up and yanked Paul to his feet and punched him over against the wall.

The last two battlers were still standing toe-to-toe. The poolhall manager said loudly, "That's plenty. Buff, step back."

Brady acted as though he were deaf, but his eyes flickered. The next moment, dozens of tiny, multicolored lights flashed brilliantly in his sight, and he fell.

The manager shuffled over to prod him with his pool cue, then to face around scowling at the three men who were stuffing in shirttails and flexing raw knuckles. One of the strangers placed two silver dollars on the green cloth of a pool table and said, "We didn't start it."

The manager looked from the strangers to the cartwheels and relaxed. But as he was shuffling over to rack up his cue he sternly said, "Clear out an' don't come back."

The strangers went over to Paul, shoving him roughly ahead of them on their way toward the doorway, and the last the manager saw of them they were turning northward still driving Paul ahead of them.

Down at the south end of town there had been another confrontation, but this one was much shorter. Neither the proprietor nor his dayman was in the runway when a husky bearded man approached reedy-voiced Alf Owens as he was saddling a horse, tapped him on the shoulder, and when Alf twisted, the husky man said, "Kind of muggy weather to be riding, friend."

Alf looked baffled.

The husky man reached past, took the horse by the reins, and without another word yanked the latigo loose, freed the flank cinch, and dumped the saddle on the ground.

Alf started to protest. The bearded man barely changed position as he lashed out with his open hand, knocked Alf against a distant horse stall, led the saddleless horse to a ring in the wall, and left him tied there by the reins. Then he went over where Alf was blinking away cobwebs. The husky man squatted, picked up Alf's hat, punched it down atop his head, and put a work-thickened big hand on Alf's shoulder. "You all right?" he asked. Alf was gingerly exploring his cheek, which was red and tender. He did not reply, so the husky man arose, still holding Alf by the shoulder, and brought him up with his back to the horse stall. His grip on Alf's shoulder tightened slightly as he asked where Alf had been going. When there was no reply the grip tightened, and continued to tighten until Alf squawked and would have pulled free except that the grip made it impossible.

"Riding out," Alf gasped, trying to lower the side of his body that was being hurt. "Who the hell are you?"

"My name's Mack. Where was you riding to?"

"Out. North was a ways. Just riding."

The grip tightened until the bone beneath the flesh was being bruised. Mack did not raise his voice. "North? Why north? Mister, I'll break your bones in a minute. Why north?"

Alf could scarcely speak because of the pain. "To find a feller."

"Mister Baxter?"

Despite the pain, Alf's eyes widened on the bearded man. "Yes. Mister Baxter."

Mack abruptly freed Alf and stood gazing thoughtfully at him. Alf sagged against the stall wall. Pain continued to spiral through his body even though the bearded man's grip was gone. He said, "Who are you?"

"I told you. My name is Mack. What's your name?"

"Alfred Owens. . . . I don't know you. Why did you—?"

"Because I don't think you ought to go up there and warn Mister Baxter."

"I wasn't goin' to warn him."

"Lyin' could get you hurt bad someday, Alf. I was in the saloon a while back. Remember?"

Alf's face congealed. He remembered. There had been three of them.

The husky man lazily rolled his head sideways. "Let's go out into the alley. We'll go up to the north end of town. I got a wagoncamp out a mile or so on a little knoll. My brothers'll be waitin' for us out there. Hand me your gun, butt first."

The bearded man methodically shucked out the loads, pocketed them, and dropped the weapon back into its holster. He gave Alf a rough slap on the injured shoulder as he said, "We're going up the alley like we're old friends."

Alf was sore and bewildered. Of one thing he was reasonably certain: he had never seen the husky man before he saw him earlier up at the saloon.

He did not speak as they went trudging up the alley with its damp earth underfoot, but his companion did. He said, "Tell me about Mister Baxter."

"Nothin' to tell. He runs a lot of cattle south of the foothills. He's got a lot of holdings and maybe six or eight riders." Alf suddenly stopped speaking and turned to stare at the husky man. "Are you a freegrazer?" he asked.

Mack smiled. "Nope. We're freighters. We've run across freegrazers though. Folks aren't real fond of them, but I got to tell you, Alf, my brothers and I don't care one way or another. We don't own no land. We camp where we got to, and sometimes cowmen run us off." Mack was still smiling as he looked down into Alf's troubled face. "What you got against freegrazers? You own grassland, do you?"

"No. When I can I ride for stockmen though."

"Alf, you take their side?" Before Alf could reply, Mack put another question to him. "Mister Baxter an' Marshal Poole pee through the same knothole, do they?"

Alf groped for an answer, found nothing he wanted to put into words, and saw the husky man's big hand coming up, so he blurted out something. "They're friends. Been friends since Marshal Poole come to the territory."

"Got cattle interests together, have they?"

"No. Denton Baxter's the cattleman. Al Poole is the town marshal."

Mack said no more. They were approaching the upper end of the alley. When they continued northward there would be nothing to prevent people from seeing them. Alf hesitated beside his companion, afraid they might meet Al Poole, and at the same time hoping they would. He had an idea what lay ahead, but what he could not understand was why this freighter, and his friends or brothers or whoever they were, were getting involved in something that had nothing to do with them. At least it had nothing to do with them as far as Alf could speculate.

They struck out again, this time going around to the rear of houses, chicken houses, and horse and milk-cow sheds on the west side of town.

It was a long walk through moist heat. Mack kept his head slightly to his right until he saw the knoll and the wagons atop it. He pointed out the camp to Alf and led off in that direction.

When they eventually got out there Alf admired the mules and several saddle animals. Evidently these freighters were careful of their animals. Not all freighters were.

A young rosy-cheeked girl popped her head out past the canvas cover near the front of one of the wagons. She had been about to call a greeting to her father. When she saw Alf, her smile faded. She pulled back out of sight and reappeared at the tailgate as her father and Alf strode past in the direction of several seated men in the shade of a waterproof texas, then scrambled down and followed at a discreet distance.

Alf stopped dead-still, staring at the man sitting cross-legged in deep shade. He said, "Paul?"

The hat brim-shaded face came up. Paul looked stonily at Alf, said nothing, and returned to his study of the black stone ring where the freighters cooked their meals.

One of the other freighters showed square teeth in a broad smile and motioned Alf to be seated near a large wagon-wheel. This freighter's face was bruised, discolored, and slightly puffy.

As Mack squatted his brothers grunted greetings and studied the man Mack had brought back with him. One of them said, "This here is Paul, Mack. Paul Sawyer. He was the only one in good enough shape after the fight at the poolhall to walk all the way out here. Paul's been tellin' us a lot of downright interestin' things." The freighter's gaze drifted to Alf. "How about this one?"

Mack eyed his youngest brother, who was lying flat out. "What happened to him?" he asked.

The man who had spoken before glanced around, then said, "He tangled with one that wouldn't quit. He'll be eatin' gruel for a day or two but he'll be all right."

The battered freighter lifted his head, winked at Mack, and sank back down.

A mongrel dog limped over to Mack and sat beside him. Mack looked over his shoulder. His daughter was beneath the wagon, eavesdropping. Mack pretended he did not see her and nudged Alf. "Tell 'em what you told me about the lawman and the cowman being partners and all."

Alf would have spoken immediately, but Paul was eyeing him coldly. Alf cleared his throat first, did not meet his friend's gaze, and told them everything he knew.

When he finished, there was a long moment of stillness, during which Annie's father whittled off a sliver of chewing tobacco and cheeked it, turned once to expectorate, then faced his brothers and said, "Started out as a friendly debt being repaid."

The bruised man propped himself up by one elbow. "There's a judge in town."

Mack nodded.

Alf surprised all but Paul by saying, "And there's a U.S. marshal in town too. I don't think they come together."

Paul mumbled, "They didn't. That marshal was here last week an' couldn't leave until the stages was runnin' again."

The three freighters slouched in thought. The dog decided to climb under the wagon where his owner was. Annie wearied of the long silence among her father and uncles, crawled back out on the far side of the wagon, got to her feet, and with the limping dog trailing along, went around to the front of the knoll where she could see the stage road, most of Harmonville, and moisture-laden heat waves farther out. It was an impressive view from Annie's point of vantage.

She was about to go back where there was wagon shade when her dog sat straight up looking northward, ears erect, eyes intent.

Annie sat down, followed out the dog's line of

sight, and saw what could be three or four horsemen walking their animals steadily in the direction of town.

She went back to the cool place beneath the wagon where her father and uncles were sitting, and announced that several riders were heading toward town from up north.

Her father stood up, looking at Alf. "Could that be them?"

Paul answered before Alf could. "It could be. If that whelp across from me hadn't walked into a damned trap like a schoolboy, had rode north like the marshal told him to, that wouldn't be Baxter."

Mack told Alf to move over against the big rear wagon-wheel beside Paul Sawyer. Mack's uninjured brother got rope and tied the prisoners with an experienced hand.

Mack gazed at his daughter fondly. "Stay away from them," he warned her. "Don't even get close enough for one of them to kick out."

She nodded.

Chapter Seventeen
A Time of Nerves

The horsemen Annie had seen were several miles above town in the direction of the foothills, and at the gait they were riding it would be a couple of hours before they got down to Harmonville.

They could have increased their gait but it was too hot and humid to ride horses any faster unless there was a good reason, and as far as Denton Baxter knew, there was no such reason.

In Harmonville humidity, less than heat, made folks droop. Among local merchants the blacksmith was the first to slacken off. He and his helper went over to the long, earthen-floored runway of the livery barn and loafed where it was cool.

Up at the general store, customers thinned out until the proprictor left his clerk in charge, crossed the back alley to the icehouse, went inside where it was bitterly cold and dark, and waited until the sweat stopped coming, then went back outside. Ten minutes later his shirt was clammily sticking to him again.

Up at the saloon, which was normally warm in winter and blessedly cool in summer, Judge Collins was slouching at a little poker table with U.S. Marshal Dallas Pierce, sipping tepid beer made palatable by peppermint. They kept a small piece of peppermint in their mouths as they sipped the beer.

Ambrose Collins was at ease. He also looked as though he had slept in his clothes, which was not unusual; he normally looked that way. He tipped ash from a cigar and considered his companion through half-closed eyes. "You're getting old," he said bluntly. "You're letting your feelings get in the way, and you damned well know better'n that."

Marshal Pierce was sitting slightly to one side in order to have room for his long legs. His reply came slowly. "Naw, that's not it, Ambrose. Maybe you're right about the age but not the rest of it. Poole's dancin' on a string that someone else is pullin'."

"Who?"

"A feller named Baxter. About the biggest rancher around here."

Judge Collins leaned to reach for his mug of beer, grunted from the effort, flopped back holding the mug, and said, "Where did you hear that?"

"A couple of places. The corralyard and up at the doctor's place. He's got a kid who's been with the freegrazers. Talkin' to those folks up there was like pulling a plug. This Baxter sent some riders to the freegrazers' camp in the night, shot one of them in the head from out in the darkness, and tried to kill the kid."

"I suppose he saw them in the dark?"

Marshal Pierce's eyes narrowed on his old friend. "You been a judge so long you wouldn't believe your own mother. The boy told me he don't really remember much. But when he was unconscious with a fever he said the name Butler. The doctor's sister heard it plain as day."

Ambrose Collins emptied his glass and pushed it away. "Let me guess," he said dryly. "Someone named Butler works for this cowman named Baxter."

Dallas Pierce smiled and nodded his head. "Butler tangled in the store here in town with the freegrazer who got bush-whacked in the dark. The freegrazer broke Butler's arm."

Judge Collins raised an arm to catch the barman's attention, then waited until refills had arrived before speaking again. "Dallas, you're trying to influence me an' you know a damned sight better than to do that."

The rawboned lawman did not smile, but his eyes twinkled. "Ambrose, we been friends upwards of fifteen years. You know I'd never try to influence you, any more'n you tried to influence me that time in the dead of winter I was settin' out to track down those bastards who shot old Judge Mosby who'd sentenced them to twenty years for killin' a clerk while robbin' a bank. You wasn't trying to influence me when you said it'd save a lot of money if they came back dead."

Ambrose Collins was looking into his beer when he replied. "I was just expressing an opinion."

Marshal Pierce looked steadily at his friend and spoke as though Judge Collins had not said a word. "And I brought them back belly-down."

Several limp townsmen came in from out front and ranged along the bar mumbling about the humidity as the barman set up their beers and put pieces of peppermint beside each glass.

Four ragged old gaffers were at a table playing matchstick poker and nursing five-cent glasses of beer. They had not been provided any peppermint and did not seem to mind being slighted.

Ambrose Collins fished out a huge tan handkerchief and swabbed his face and neck, then carelessly stuffed it into a coat pocket with half of it hanging out. "I got to hold court," he mumbled, looking at something beyond Marshal Pierce's right shoulder.

The lawman nodded.

Judge Collins's gaze returned to his old friend's face. "I can put it off for a day, or I can remand these freegrazers to their cells on the grounds that Mister Poole needs more evidence; there's always a loophole."

Marshal Pierce nodded again.

His Honor sighed and struggled up out of his chair, hitched at his sagging britches, and without another word headed for the roadway, leaving the marshal to finish his beer and suck on the peppermint.

The sun was high in a flawless turquoise sky. The heat seemed to have lost some of its humidity as Judge Collins went northward to the Harmonville firehouse, where someone had stuck a national flag into a bucket of sand and had arranged an old table near the rear of the room in front of the flag. There were six or seven wooden benches a few yards in front of the table. Judge Collins made his inspection, tried the rickety chair behind the table, then walked out into the sunshine. He had two law books, a gavel, and a Bible among his belongings down at the roominghouse. He had not opened any of the books in a long time; he carried them along because they lent substance to his position when he convened court. Like the flag, they were an essential part of his trappings of judicial office.

His presence in Harmonville had been noted the day before. People knew who were in the jailhouse cells. Every time a judge arrived in town to hold court, discussions livened the day. Sometimes the discussions got heated. This particular occasion was no different.

Barry Haliday, who managed the corralyard for the company up in Denver that owned the stage line, was ambivalent in what he said about the freegrazers. If they had not saved his horses and coach he would have been outspokenly hostile to them, but now he seemed to agree with his yardmen, who had also witnessed Charley Waite's behavior at the height of the storm, that freegrazer or not, Waite had done something heroic. His yardmen were not cowmen either, and even though they could not have avoided some of the hostility to freegrazers that had rubbed off on most people, today they considered freegrazing as much less of a transgression because of what that freegrazer had done for them at the height of the storm.

Barry was a wispy, unsmiling man, strong on religion and fiercely opposed to both whiskey and gambling. He was out front with his corralyard foreman, a large Mexican, when he saw Judge Collins striding in the direction of the firehouse with his Bible and law books. He watched His

Honor's progress. The large Mexican sucked his teeth and also watched, but he was not inhibited and spoke frankly. "They put people on trial for trying to make a living and when it is over with, the prisoner ends up with the rope and the law gets his cow."

Barry made a little sniffing sound. Judge Collins had turned abruptly to enter the saloon. Barry said, "It's the devil's business," and walked back into the corralyard with the Mexican following him.

Down the roadway on the same side, Marshal Poole missed seeing His Honor. He was leaning on his desk scowling at a pair of battered townsmen. "Why," he asked for the third time, "would they take Paul away with them?"

Buff Brady gave the same reply he'd offered before. "All I know is that when I come around, Hugh Fenwick told me that's what they done."

Marshal Poole tapped on the tabletop. He eyed big George Kendal but did not address him. There was rarely any reason to question George; his best answers were invariably formed by a ten-year-old intelligence.

Brady ached. "Fenwick said he'd seen 'em in town before."

Marshal Poole left his chair to go draw off a cup of black coffee from the woodstove and take it to one of the little barred front-wall windows. With his back to his vigilantes he said, "What in hell did they want with Paul? There are always fights an' when they're over someone goes up to Doc's place to get patched up." He turned to face into the room. "Fellers get into a fight they don't take the loser off with them. Why Paul? Why not one of you?"

Brady answered dully. "Mister Fenwick said Paul gave up. Me an' George was plumb out of it. To take us with 'em they'd have had to carry us."

Marshal Poole returned to his chair, still gripping the coffee cup. "Have either of you seen Alf?"

They hadn't. George brightened when he said, "He was lucky he wasn't in the poolhall."

Marshal Poole drank the cup half empty before putting it aside. He did not tell them he had sent Alf north to intercept Denton Baxter; he told them instead to go on home and clean up, that they looked as if they'd been dragged the full length of Main Street behind a scouring mule.

When he was alone Marshal Poole stared at the ceiling for a long time, then went over to the cell-room door, unbarred it, and walked down to halt in the pale gloom, eyeing his prisoners.

This time it was Charley who was sleeping and Boss who was awake sitting on the side of his bunk. Poole said, "There was you, that feller sleeping, the kid, and the big feller who's dead. Right?"

Boss nodded.

Poole looked at Charley. "Who are your friends in town?"

"Don't have any," Boss replied. "About the only folks we know are the doctor an' his sister."

Marshal Poole continued to gaze at the inert man on the wall bunk for a moment or two, then swung and walked back up to his office.

He had an intuitive feeling, too vague and illusory to be pinned down for examination, but it was nevertheless in the back of his mind, and it would not go away.

Something was going on.

The roadway door opened. Judge Collins filled

the opening looking sweaty and rumpled, with part of a tan handkerchief hanging out of a coat pocket. He said, "I'll be at the firehouse whenever you are ready, marshal. If you got the facts written down I could take them up there to study while you're gettin' the chains on 'em."

Poole went to the desk, picked up a four-page handwritten complaint, and handed it to His Honor as he said, "You know that federal marshal who's in town?"

Collins was perusing the papers in his hands when he replied. "Dallas Pierce? I've known him a long time." His Honor's testy eyes lifted. "Some coincidence, him being stuck here until the roads got hard again, and me arriving when I did."

Al Poole muttered. "Yeah, some coincidence. All right, I'll get the chains on 'em and march 'em up there in a little while."

Judge Collins stood gazing steadily at the town marshal for a long time, then turned and closed the jailhouse door after himself.

As Marshal Poole went after his leg and wrist irons in the storeroom, Judge Collins was crossing the roadway squinting in the direction of a rangy, large man leaning on an upright post in front of the general store, watching the jailhouse. His Honor stopped a yard short of the plankwalk, looked up, and said, "I'm authorized to spend five dollars for a bailiff."

The U.S. marshal smiled faintly while studying the sweaty, fleshy face in front of him. "You don't need a bailiff, Ambrose."

His Honor did not relent. "You never know, Dallas." He rocked his head backward to indicate the jailhouse. "Something is bothering him."

Pierce's rejoinder was as dry as corn husks. "Maybe it's his conscience."

Collins stepped up into the shade before speaking again. "You been here long enough to start gettin' influenced." Dallas Pierce looked at the shorter man. "I only figured there was somethin' wrong, starting with yesterday." He looked northward up the roadway. "You can find another bailiff. I'd kind of like to stand out here and watch for this cowman."

Judge Collins swiveled his head northward. "He's coming for a fact?"

"Not for a fact. No one told me he was. But I been at this trade a long time. If the town marshal is goin' to bring culprits before your court, an' the basis of his charges against these culprits arises from trouble with this feller Baxter, I'd expect Mister Baxter to show up to support the town marshal's charges."

Judge Collins held his coat open to catch as much of a little stray breeze as he could. Marshal Pierce brought forth a thin, dark cigar from an inside coat pocket, offered it to the judge, who shook his head, so Pierce lighted up, trickled smoke, and without looking down again, said, "Ambrose, if just half of what I've heard the last day or so is true, just half of it, mind you, that town marshal over yonder and his friend named Baxter are so crooked that when they die, folks will have to screw them into the ground."

Ambrose Collins fished out his tan handkerchief to mop off sweat, and as carelessly as before, shoved it back into a coat pocket. "Dallas, you be careful. As far as I know right now, even if the town marshal is up to something, an' even if his partner the cowman comes into town, this here is a routine case of assault."

The federal officer continued to smoke his stogie, lean against the overhang upright, and alternately watch the northward roadway and His Honor, who was marching up toward the firehouse.

Chapter Eighteen
In the Middle of the Road!

Marshal Poole brought his prisoners up to the jailhouse office and told Charley to go sit on a bench and stay there while he clamped leg irons on Boss Spearman, then belted him with a midriff chain and cuffed both his wrists to it. Boss couldn't even scratch if he got an itch.

He did not say a word. Neither did Charley when it was his turn to be shackled, but when the lawman went to a rack for a short-barreled shotgun, which he methodically loaded in their sight, Charley said, "If this is what you do to men who haven't done anything but defend themselves, what do you do to murderers?"

Poole ignored Charley to open the roadway door while facing inward. He jerked his head for them to leave the room and made a curt announcement. "Just walk across the road an' turn north. I'll tell you when to stop. I'll be behind you. If you try to duck down between any buildings, I'll blow you in half. Move!"

They both faltered when blinding sunlight struck their faces. Charley rattled his chains as he nudged Boss to keep him walking. It seemed improbable that Poole would kill them in plain sight of startled onlookers on both sides of Main Street, but every graveyard west of the Missouri River held evidence that this was nothing to gamble on.

People stopped to watch, mostly in silence, but occasionally to murmur to each other. Marshal Poole had his shotgun in the crook of one arm. He looked neither right nor left. When they were passing the general store and a startled man said, "They couldn't run if they wanted to," the town marshal snarled at him.

There were some rangemen tying horses at the rack in front of the saloon. They became motionless as they watched the clanking cavalcade approach. One rangeman leaned down on the hitchrack, smiling. He was about to say something about sonofabitching freegrazers when a tall, rangy, older man walking ten feet behind Marshal Poole spoke sharply. "Keep your damned mouth shut!"

Al Poole gave a little start, risked a fast rearward stare, recognized the U.S. marshal, and faced forward again as he growled at the federal officer. "What the hell do you think you're doing?"

They were past the staring, motionless rangemen before Dallas Pierce replied. "Bringing up the rear."

There was a small crowd out front of the firehall. Judge Collins was among them, tan handkerchief hanging from a coat pocket. Marshal

Poole said, "Spearman! Waite! Turn in up there. Stay close together and don't stop!"

Among the onlookers in front of the improvised courtroom were two older men wearing stained riders' coats that reached below their knees. Neither the heat nor the diminishing humidity appeared to bother them. The federal marshal recognized them and nodded as he went past. He had passed some uncomfortable hours with them on the southbound stage, talking about the cattle business. They were livestock buyers. They nodded back, and after everyone else was inside the firehall, they too entered the building, removed greasy old hats, and sought seats on the benches.

Judge Collins stood leaning on the back of his chair. When Marshal Poole pushed Waite and Spearman down with the butt of his shotgun, Judge Collins said, "Mister Poole, put that scattergun aside."

The town marshal reddened as he moved toward a chair and placed the gun across it. He glared at the judge, but Ambrose Collins was seating himself, arranging his coat, and did not look back. He waited a moment or two until the room was quiet, then he said, "Which of you is Boss Spearman?"

Boss nodded his head.

Collins eyed Charley. "Then you'll be Mister Waite."

Charley neither spoke nor nodded.

Judge Collins leaned on the table for a moment gazing at them, then he said, "Mister Poole, take the chains off them."

The town marshal protested. "Your Honor,

these men tried to kill some range riders in the night."

His Honor tilted his jaw toward the roadway doors farther back where Dallas Pierce was indolently leaning. "If they can get past Mister Pierce back there, I'll let them go. Take the chains off."

Poole got keys from his pocket and approached the prisoners at the same time the roadway door opened and a woman, a man, and a gangling boy entered. Dallas Pierce pointed to seats and closed the door behind them.

A moment later, while Marshal Poole was freeing Charley after having already let Boss's chains fall to the floor, the roadway door opened again. This time a wispy, vinegary-faced man accompanied by a very large Mexican and three other men came in. Dallas Pierce pointed them to benches and closed the door.

Poole returned to his seat beside the spare chair where his scattergun rested. Boss scratched and Charley rubbed his wrists.

His Honor held up some papers. "Gents, the charges against you include attempted murder, trespassing, assault, resistin' arrest, and defyin' the law." Collins put the papers down and leaned back in his rickety chair. "I don't know whether you ever been through something like this before, so I'll explain it to you. If you plead guilty I'll try you here and now. If you plead innocent, I'll call this a preliminary hearing, listen to everything you got to say, then decide whether you should be held over for a formal trial an' sentencing. How do you plead, Mister Spearman?"

Boss hung fire but eventually said, "Judge, it ain't that simple. One of my men was bushwhacked and killed and another feller—"

"Hold it," exclaimed His Honor. "First things first. Whichever way you plead you'll get a full hearing, but I want to know whether we'll be holding a hearing or a trial. Guilty or not guilty, Mister Spearman?"

"Not guilty, Your Honor."

Collins rocked forward and planted fleshy arms on the table as he looked over where the town marshal was sitting. "All right. This here will be a hearing, Marshal Poole. . . . Hold it! Just listen and don't interrupt. That's the law. You don't have to like it. Lots of times I don't like the law. But you an' I both serve it, an' you've been through this many times, so you darned well know what the routine is."

His Honor struck the tabletop with his gavel, leaned forward gazing around the room, looking longest back where Marshal Pierce was leaning, then rustled the papers in front of him and announced that his court was now in session to hear charges against one Boss Spearman and one Charley Waite.

His Honor leaned back again, studying faces among the laden benches, then cleared his throat to speak when the roadway door was opened and several men pushed inside. His Honor frowned at this interruption. After the intruders were seated, he called toward the rear of the room. "Marshal Pierce, lock that door, will you?"

"Your Honor, there isn't any inside lock."

"Well, find a chair and put it against the door."

While the U.S. marshal was doing this, Judge Collins glanced from the prisoners to the town marshal. Al Poole was sitting twisted from the waist, staring at the men who had just entered. His face was white.

He had recognized two of those five newcomers: Alf Owens and Paul Sawyer.

The judge cleared his pipes again and launched forward to lean on the table and clasp both hands as he gazed at the town marshal. "Mister Poole, I've studied your complaint. It seems to be in order. You mention a Mister Baxter in it several times. I'd like to ask you a question: Since Mister Baxter is the complainant, why isn't he here? Of course I can hold a hearin' without a complainant as long as there's a signed complaint like this one you wrote up an' signed, but when it comes to questioning, your case could darned well suffer without the complainant being here to support and elaborate on the charges. Where is this gent?"

Marshal Poole's reply was barely audible. "He ranches near the foothills north of town, Your Honor. It's a long ride at a time of the year when stockmen are real busy."

His Honor continued to slouch forward throughout a long period of silence, gazing at the town marshal. He eventually leaned back to range a searching glance toward the rear of the room.

The U.S. marshal was smiling.

Marshal Poole had been desperately thinking. He now said, "Your Honor, if the court wishes, we can lock the prisoners back in their cell an' I can ride out to find Mister Baxter and most likely get back here with him in the morning."

Judge Collins looked annoyed. "You should have sent for him when you knew I was in town, marshal. I got a schedule. Harmonville is only one of my stops. Now I got to waste another day, an' that'll throw me behind all the way down the line."

Al Poole was not thinking of the judge's inconvenience, but of two related factors. One was Alf sitting back there with Paul. He knew Paul had been abducted by those men who had started the fight at the poolhall. Obviously they had caught Alf too, before he could head north to warn Denton Baxter not to arrive in Harmonville.

The other factor was that note Baxter had sent him telling him to leave town and stay away all night, which had meant that Baxter and at least his best gunhands intended to reach Harmonville, probably in the dark, kill his freegraze prisoners, and escape in the darkness.

Judge Collins struggled to stand up, struck the tabletop with his gavel, and said, "This hearing will be postponed until nine o'clock tomorrow morning."

Dallas Pierce opened the roadway doors and stepped aside so the first spectators could return to the roadway. Marshal Poole picked up his shotgun and pushed past to leave quickly. His Honor walked back and met the U.S. marshal as the last of the onlookers cleared the doors. He said, "Satisfied?"

Dallas Pierce did not commit himself. "I'll lay you five to one he don't bring Baxter back."

"You thought Baxter would ride in. That's what you told me in front of the general store. Well?"

Dallas Pierce said, "Ambrose, I've been wrong about as often as I've been right, and so have you. I'm goin' down to the cafe."

Collins fished for his tan handkerchief. It was hot in the firehouse. "I'll meet you at the saloon after dark." He turned back to retrieve his three books and his gavel.

Marshal Poole left the cuffs, chains, and leg irons on the firehouse floor and herded his prisoners quickly through the lingering crowd out front, down in the direction of the jailhouse.

Harmonville was quiet, with no buggy or wagon traffic; most of the pedestrians were still up in front of the firehouse. The afternoon was wearing along. Down in front of the general store the proprietor and his clerk were rolling barrels back inside the store from out front, and farther down, out front of the livery barn, several men were slouching in tree shade, watching the front of the firehouse at the opposite end of town.

They saw Al Poole herding his prisoners. A man with a bandaged arm leaned to speak to another man. They conversed briefly, then the man with the injured arm turned to give a quick order to a rider, who immediately darted back down into the livery barn.

Another of the four men ran swiftly into the barn and returned carrying a Winchester carbine. He knelt as Marshal Poole and his prisoners were approaching the center of the road.

Someone up there called to Poole. He ordered his prisoners to stand still and turned as the rangy U.S. marshal strode up and said, "Are you going to ride north tonight?"

Poole nodded. "Yeah. Get something to eat, then head out."

Dallas Pierce said, "I'll ride with you."

Al Poole stared unblinkingly at the federal officer. "No need."

"You never can tell, Mister Poole. You're most likely right. Then again, if this Mister Baxter don't want to ride back, maybe I can talk him into it. You're a town marshal. You got authority here in Harmonville. I'm a federal marshal. I got authority anywhere."

Al Poole's hand holding the shotgun was sweating. Dallas Pierce's expression said very plainly that he was going whether Al Poole liked the idea or not. "All right. I'll lock the prisoners up and meet you over at the cafe. You can rent a horse at the livery barn."

Marshal Poole was turning toward his prisoners, who had not moved but who had overheard the conversation between the lawmen, and the federal marshal was starting to turn away when the gunshot sounded. Boss Spearman staggered, raised a hand, and fell.

Dallas Pierce dropped to one knee, swept his right hand back and downward, then forward as he pulled back the weapon's hammer.

The gunman at the lower end of town was a moving blur in tree shade when Pierce fired at him. The man disappeared into the livery barn.

People were crying out and running in all directions. Two of them ran directly toward the men in the center of the roadway. Marshal Poole stood holding his scattergun, staring southward. Pierce yelled at him and ran across in front of Poole heading for a vacant place between buildings on his way toward the back alley. Poole did not move. He seemed to be in a trance, even when Doctor Barlow called him to help carry Boss Spearman out of the roadway.

Charley lunged at the shotgun, yanked it from Poole's grip, and ran after the federal officer.

From the plankwalk opposite the firehouse two large men also went flinging westward toward the alley, leaving another large man to watch Alf and Paul. He was not pleased to be burdened with them, so he roughly shoved them down the roadway toward the jailhouse, and passed the doctor, his sister, an ashen-faced youth, and four townsmen who were carrying Boss Spearman up to the doctor's cottage.

Marshal Poole finally got untracked and was in front of his jailhouse when the burly freighter shouldered him aside and drove his prisoners inside. When Poole entered the freighter said, "Lock them in, and they better be here when I get back." Then he too ran around toward the alley.

Chapter Nineteen
Ahead of Dawn

Marshal Pierce knew someone had been running behind him, and as he squinted toward the lower end of town in time to see dust rising, he spoke without looking around. "They're getting away. Hell, there was four or five of them."

Charley did not stop. He was moving past Dallas Pierce carrying the scattergun when he replied. "Baxter, sure as hell."

Pierce recognized Al Poole's prisoner from the courtroom. "Hey! Where the hell do you think you're going!"

Charley broke over into a trot toward the lower end of town as he answered. "I'm going after them."

Marshal Pierce started to yell something else, then checked himself and broke over into a clumsy lope to keep up with Charley Waite.

The noise and confusion around in front was

audible to the running pair in the alley even after they reached the livery barn from out back and rushed in to cause a startled hostler to squawk and begin gesticulating. "They run south!"

Charley ignored that. "Fetch two good horses. Move, damn it!"

The hostler jumped as though he'd been stung, grabbed shanks from a wall peg, and scuttled for the horses. For the first time Dallas Pierce had a chance to say something without yelling it to his companion.

"We need a few more riders."

Charley was agitated and impatient. He went looking for the hostler as he said, "Go get them. Waste time if you want to. Me, I'm goin' to catch that son of a bitch if I got to chase him to hell and for two days over the coals!"

The hostler returned from out back with two strongly put-together bay horses, neither of which would have won beauty contests, but each had muscle in the right amounts in the right places.

Saddling and bridling was done expertly and swiftly. At the last moment the hostler said, "Mister, you ain't really goin' after them with a shotgun, are you? Wait a minute."

The hostler disappeared into the harness room and almost immediately returned with a saddle-gun, which he handed to Charley, who was astride. Charley nodded. "I'm obliged," he said, and tossed the shotgun to the ground, whirled, and led off out into the alleyway with Marshal Pierce following.

Charley rode southward only until he had open country on his right, then turned west, holding his powerful bay horse to a lope. Dallas Pierce protested. "What the hell! You heard him say they went south!"

Charley turned to look steadily at the rawboned older man. "Did you ever hunt cattle, marshal?" He raised an arm pointing westward. "You do it by the smell of dust."

Dallas Pierce lapsed into silence, occasionally eyeing his companion, who had to ride balancing the hostler's carbine across his lap because he had no saddleboot.

A half hour later with dusk foreshortening visibility, the marshal dryly said, "I hope you got a good nose, Mister Waite. At the rate they'll be traveling, with nightfall a couple of hours off, we could damned well lose them."

Charley rode in silence. He knew they had gone west, and it was beginning to dawn on him why they had, but he rode in silence.

A couple of times the lawman looked back or cocked his head to listen. Charley shook his head. "If anyone's coming, marshal, I'd guess they listened to that hostler and are heading south."

After a while, as they were covering ground at a lope, Pierce swore with disgust. "If that was Baxter, why did he shoot the old man?"

"Didn't anyone tell you that Baxter's done this before? Rounded up freegraze cattle while their owners was either locked up or scairt out of the country—or maybe shot like happened to Boss—drove the cattle out of the country and sold them?"

Pierce nodded slowly. "The lady up at the doctor's place mentioned something like that."

"And you didn't believe her?"

"Well, you may be able to follow a trail by the smell of roiled dust, but in my business, Mister

Waite, we learn real early that when folks are upset and agitated they say just about anything that pops into their heads."

Charley rode steadily without picking up the gait; a loping horse can cover three times as much ground as a running horse. When they eventually slackened off he changed course slightly. Dallas Pierce noticed but had come to rely on his companion's initiative and did not comment.

Darkness arrived with a sickle moon and winking stars. They could see no more than a hundred yards ahead. Pierce finally mentioned an ambush. Charley shrugged. "Yeah, maybe. But I don't think so. Baxter's heading straight for the open country out where we had our cattle. The rest of his riders will be out there. Maybe they been out there for the last couple of days rounding up the cattle that got scattered by the storm."

Marshal Pierce's brows dropped a notch. "How many men's he got?"

Charley was not certain. "I'd guess about eight or ten." He saw the rawboned lawman purse his lips. "Mister Waite, I was in front of the store back in town waiting for Baxter to show up."

"You didn't see them?"

"No. Well, when Poole herded you two up toward the firehouse it looked to me like he might shoot you, so I sort of fell in behind and worried him a little."

Charley angled slightly more northward again. "How came you to be interested?" he asked.

"The doctor and his sister told me a story. So did that vinegary old coot who runs the corralyard. And the feller who owns the saloon. After a while when you've heard pretty much the same thing from several people, you sort of fit the parts together. I've been at this business a long time."

To their right a cow bawled, in among some trees. Charley gazed up there until they had passed the area. The only cattle out here had been Boss's, but this critter was no less than ten miles from where the wagoncamp had been. Maybe all the cattle had not fled west ahead of the storm. He'd look into this when he had the opportunity.

They loped four more miles, halted where they frightened some wild animal out of its bed, listened to its bounding flight, then swung off to slip bridles, loosen cinches, and allow the pair of bays to pick for a while. They had not seemed tired, but a little rest wouldn't hurt.

Marshal Pierce offered Charley a cigar, which Waite declined. As the lawman lit up inside his hat he said, "We're halfway?"

Charley nodded. "Close to it. It was a long day's wagon ride down to Harmonville. On saddle animals a man could peel off about a third of that. We'd ought to be out there before dawn. We'd better be, because there isn't even a big rock or a decent tree out there."

Pierce sat on the ground trickling smoke and eyeing the high rash of stars. "I'd feel a lot better if those townsmen hadn't gone south." He dropped ash before continuing. "Odds are somethin' a man in my business is really ticklish about."

Charley smiled sardoncially. "And nowhere to hide. Not a tree until you get a mile or so beyond where we had our camp, then it's a piddlin' creek with willows."

"Mister Waite, you got a real knack for makin' a man feel good."

Charley would have laughed, but he had the

vivid image fixed squarely behind his eyes of the way Boss had fallen after the bullet hit him.

A coyote yelped and fled from the scent of humans. Other coyotes were also out there; they also fled but did not sound.

Charley went after his horse and was slipping the bridle into place when Marshal Pierce led his bay over and said, "You know the country; how are we goin' to get up to them if there's no cover?"

Charley was snugging up the cinch when he answered. "By tryin' to reach their camp before sunrise."

"Where will it be?"

Charley swung up over leather. "By the creek. That's the only water out there."

"Where along the creek?"

Charley was reining away as he answered curtly, "I don't know. We'll have to find it."

The bays were right up there in the bit. The rest had helped, but they hadn't actually needed it. They were in good condition, young enough to be stout with lots of "bottom" and old enough not to act coltish.

The night was pleasantly cool. It was also inhabited by a variety of nocturnal creatures, most of whom picked up man scent well in advance and simply were not there when the riders loped by. A dog-wolf was in a spit of trees, where he could make out the intruders riding past. He watched them out of sight, then tipped his head back and made a mournful howl.

Charley had landmarks to go by, but only as long as the land was uneven or timbered. When he was finally passing over very gently undulating country without a tree in sight, he told the lawman they were no more than two or three miles from his old wagoncamp, beyond which was the willow creek.

From this point on they did not lope.

Charley studied the eastern horizon by sitting twisted in the saddle with his palm flat down on the bay horse's rump. There was no sign of daybreak, but it was not far off because the night was beginning to feel chilly.

Marshal Pierce rubbed his hands together and swung both arms. He had a perfectly serviceable rider's coat in his room back at Harmonville. To kill time he asked about Mose Harrison. Charley told him of finding Mose dead with a shattered skull. He also told him where they had buried Mose, and a short while later when they passed the spot, he pointed out the grave.

After that they said very little, finally drifting off into silence, and paced through the chilly late night—or early morning—concentrating on what was ahead.

They had made excellent time getting out here. Better time than Charley had thought possible, but whatever they did now would have to be done promptly. They had left the last vestige of shelter far behind; from now on they would be clearly visible after daylight arrived.

They angled northward, saw creek willows, paralleled them for a mile, and when they halted as Marshal Pierce leaned to speak, Charley silenced him with an upraised hand. He turned back the way they had come to begin exploring southward.

Only one thing mattered to Charley now: Find Baxter's camp. Beyond that he had only a vague idea of what to do. He was a stockman, not a manhunter. He had never stalked anyone before in his life.

Pierce's bay horse missed his lead, recovered, and continued onward with both ears forward and his head up. The marshal hissed at Charley, swung to the ground, and moved to the bay's head to keep it from nickering.

Both men stood ready to stifle a nicker. They could see nothing nor detect a scent, but clearly their horses had detected something ahead through the darkness that held their attention.

Pierce shoved his reins into Charley's hand and scouted ahead. Within two minutes Charley could not see him. It was not a long wait, although it seemed to be.

Marshal Pierce came soundlessly out of the gloom, wagged his head, and spoke quietly. "I think maybe you were right. I don't know whether it's Baxter or not, but there's a roundup camp down there. No wagon but a rope corral of horses an' as near as I could make out, maybe eight or so men in their soogans."

As Pierce retrieved his reins he indicated that this was something he knew a little about. "We don't have a hell of a lot of time. We can sneak up and set there with cocked pistols to maybe take them without trouble when they awaken."

Charley shook his head. "Not Baxter."

"All right. Here, hold my horse again. I'll cut their corral rope and stampede the horses. I'd guess they're a hell of a distance from getting more saddle stock. . . . Mister Waite, you'd better take the horses back up the creek a ways and stay in among the willows. Sure as hell those horses will run for it, and that'll bring those men up out of their blankets like hitting a hornet's nest with a stick. I hope they'll think the rope broke. It's too dark for them to find my tracks. All the same, you get hid up yonder."

Charley eyed the rawboned older man. "Baxter and the fellers who was with him down in Harmonville couldn't have got back here very long ago. My guess is that some of them won't be asleep. They'll have someone standin' watch down there, marshal."

Dallas Pierce smiled without humor. "I'll be careful. Mister Waite, this isn't somethin' I haven't done before."

Pierce turned away. Charley watched him out of sight, then started walking northward over beside the creek. If something went wrong, and something usually did even when lives weren't at stake, he and the U.S. marshal were about as vulnerable as men could be.

He kept walking, the bays trailing him on slack reins, heads down and relaxed.

They started up a horned owl, who normally soared in total silence, but this time he made whispery sounds by frantically beating his wings to hasten his escape.

When Charley thought he might have covered a decent distance, better than a half mile, he began searching for a place to get in among the creek willows. What he eventually found was a place where there were no willows; the creek was wider up here with a shallow bottom. Charley had found an animal crossing. Over the years indifferent bodies and sharp hooves had killed out willow shoots to a width of about fifteen feet.

He led the bays in there. The ground was spongy. Both horses pulled for slack and began nipping off tender willow shoots.

Charley had time to reflect on his fierce rush for vengeance. It might have been wiser to round up some possemen, even though that would have cost valuable time. What convinced him that it could not have been done was the basic fact that he had been a prisoner of the law back in Harmonville. Men would not have followed him; they would have handed him over to Marshal Poole.

In the utter hush of predawn, a slow-gathering accumulation of reverberations underfoot—running horses—told him that Dallas Pierce had been successful; he had put Baxter's crew on foot.

Charley did not feel especially elated. Dawn was no more than an hour off. After daylight arrived Baxter would find boot tracks and a cut rope instead of a frayed, broken one.

Chapter Twenty
Through Darkness Toward Dawn

When Marshal Pierce found the animal-crossing he stood a while sucking down deep sweeps of air. He was sweating. Charley waited patiently until the lawman caught his breath from running.

"I cut the rope in back, to the west, and their horses ran that way when they discovered they were loose. Maybe they'll find tracks, but not by the corral." Pierce lifted his hat, pushed sweat off with a soiled cuff and replaced the hat, then held out a hand for his reins. He did not say any more until he had led the way eastward from the creek in a big, half-mile-deep half circle. Out where he halted facing the direction of an aroused camp, he smiled at Charley. "You're goin' to earn your keep from here on," he said. He swung to the ground, unbuckled one rein, and fashioned Mormon hobbles with it.

Charley did the same. When Pierce started walking in the direction of the shouting and cursing, Charley was beside him carrying the livery barn nighthawk's Winchester.

The cursing was subsiding by the time Pierce and Waite were close enough to dimly make out moving silhouettes. They halted, sank low, and listened to an angry man giving orders.

"Couple of you trail 'em. Arch, you'n Slim head in the direction of the yard. Someone's got to catch at least one horse and bring him back here."

A man replied to these orders with a question. "Mister Baxter, wasn't that new rope?"

The angry man retorted shortly. "Yeah, but ropes break. You fellers get moving. I'll go over the rope."

The same voice that had spoken before had something else to say. "Supposin' a posse comes out here, Mister Baxter?"

This time the angry man exploded. He swore fiercely at the other speaker, then yelled at him. "Gawddammit, start walking! Take ropes or bridles, but get the hell on the trail of those horses."

For a while the camp was quiet except for men moving, scuffing the ground, rummaging among saddlebags, or making momentary match flares as they lighted smokes.

Marshal Pierce leaned to nudge Charley. "That's what I admire, Mister Waite. A cooperative son of a bitch. Four men goin' after horses. Two of 'em goin' in the wrong direction. How many you reckon he's got left?"

Charley didn't guess. "More than two, marshal, an' daylight's coming."

Dallas Pierce looked eastward, arose to yank

loose the tiedown over his holstered Colt, and started to slowly pick a path closer to the camp. Charley drifted off to one side. He did not know whether Dallas Pierce was one of those shoot-it-out lawmen or not, and he did not intend to be close to him if he turned out to be one.

They could see each other faintly. Up ahead a man with a growly voice said, "Suppose I didn't kill the son of a bitch?"

Baxter's identifiable voice answered brusquely. "You killed him. I've seen 'em go down like that before an' they never got up again."

A lighter voice spoke. Charley thought this speaker was younger than his companions. "That was a good lick, blindfolding that liveryman. He not only didn't see any of our faces, but he was so scairt I thought he'd wet his pants."

Baxter growled at the younger man. "See if there're any coals left. Stir up something so's we can have breakfast."

Charley concentrated on the place where the man with the growly voice had spoken. This was the man he had come out here to settle with for the shooting of Boss Spearman.

Without warning, a striding rider appeared through the gloom in Charley's direction. He would pass less than five feet away. There was no way he could avoid seeing Charley.

There was not very much time to react. Charley got both legs positioned so he could spring up, gripping the carbine tightly, until the silhouette got so close he could see a soiled bandage on the man's arm, then came up off the ground as he cocked the Winchester.

The man wearing the bandage stopped so

abruptly he nearly tripped. Charley heard his quick intake of breath.

He approached the astonished rider, pushed his gunbarrel into the man's stomach, and whispered to him, "Not a sound." The rider wore an ivory-stocked six-gun on the same side as his bandaged arm. Charley lifted it from the holster and used it to gesture in the direction he wanted the rider to walk.

When they got over where the lawman had been, he was not there. Charley knocked his prisoner unconscious with the man's own gun, knelt to gag him and lash his arms and ankles, then sat back considering the rider. He thought this was the man who had shot Mose Harrison. He certainly was one of the men Mose had fought with in the store down in Harmonville. He had to be the man whose arm Mose had broken. His name would be Butler.

Marshal Pierce appeared without a sound. He gazed at the man, whose hat had been punched violently down to his ears when Charley had knocked him senseless.

He hunkered down, took the ivory-handled Colt from Charley, and held it close to his face examining it before he said, "I know him. I know this gun. He's Ed Carlin, wanted for murder in Montana and Idaho." Pierce handed back the weapon and stood up. "Mister Waite, we got to assume Baxter's got maybe another hired gunfighter over there. . . . You go south, I'll go north. You get flat down on your belly, an' when I call Baxter, don't be a hero. Hold off until you're fired at or I'm fired at, then just pick a target and shoot."

Charley arose looking eastward. Finally, there

was a thin wedge of soiled gray limning the farthest horizon. He walked away from Marshal Pierce without a word, intending to indeed find a target—the man with the deep, growly voice.

A spindly little flicker of fire came to life amid the jumble of camp and horse gear. It reflected off three men. One of them was Denton Baxter; Charley remembered him from their first meeting in the marshal's office.

Another man was tall and thin. He moved with the grace and ease of youth. He would be the one with the young voice. Charley settled flat down with the Winchester pushed ahead, studying the man farthest from him, stooping over to paw through saddlebags. He was about Baxter's age but hadn't run as much to fat as yet. He looked dark by feeble firelight. Charley concentrated on him. By the process of elimination this had to be the growly voiced man who had mentioned the possibility of his shot not having killed Boss Spearman.

Charley slowly snugged back the Winchester and waited.

Marshal Pierce must have taken plenty of time to get into position before challenging the camp. Charley was beginning to wonder if he was ever going to do it, when the lawman sang out.

"Don't move! Don't even breathe! Now straighten up and toss away those guns with your left hands!"

None of the surprised men near the little fire had moved since Pierce's first word. Baxter turned his head in the direction of the lawman's voice. Charley could see his features clearly; they were twisted with equal parts surprise and defiance.

Charley eased back the Winchester's hammer. It made almost no noise, certainly not enough to reach the utterly still men by the fire.

It wasn't Baxter who precipitated what followed, but the thick-bodied dark man. He dropped and rolled. Charley squeezed the trigger. His muzzleblast stopped the gangling younger man dead still with his hand inches above his gun grip.

The dark man arched up off the ground as though to whip around facing southward. Charley shot him again, levered up, and shot him a third time. Each slug rocked the heavy body.

Baxter dove across the fire to land in the midst of camp boxes and mounded horse equipment.

Charley did not take his eyes off the man he had shot as Marshal Pierce fired three times with his six-gun. The shots were so closely spaced they sounded like one continuous drumroll of muzzleblast as they ripped into Baxter's hiding place.

Echoes spiraled violently in all directions. They were still audible, but just barely, when Marshal Pierce called to the younger man. "Shuck the gun!"

The rider very slowly lifted out his weapon and let it fall. Then he sank to the ground in a slump.

Neither Charley nor Dallas Pierce arose for a long while, and before they did Pierce ordered the younger man to drag Denton Baxter to the fire.

After that had been done and there was clear evidence that Baxter was dead, the dark man was also dead, and the remaining rider was completely demoralized, Marshal Pierce stood up, cocked six-gun in his right fist, and walked slowly toward the camp.

Charley watched without moving. Pierce went over to nudge the dead men with a boot toe, looked down at the man on the ground with his face in his hands, and called softly. "Fetch in the other one, Mister Waite."

Charley got stiffly upright with the Winchester at his side and walked away from the camp southward. The man he had hit over the head was conscious; he didn't blink as he watched Charley walk up.

Charley knelt to free the man's ankles. Then he pulled him to his feet, half turned him, untied the gag, and punched him toward the campfire. They hadn't covered twenty feet when his prisoner said, "What happened?"

"Your boss is dead. So is that son of a bitch who shot Boss Spearman in Harmonville, and you're teetering on the edge."

Marshal Pierce had emptied the pockets of the dead men into their hats. He had found a bottle of whiskey and was squatting across from the youngest rider, sipping. When the other survivor came into the light, Pierce looked up at him for a long time before speaking.

"Carlin. We come pretty close to meeting once before, near Laramie up in Wyoming."

The prisoner looked at the dead men and at the young man who was still covering his face with both hands. Charley growled for him to sit down, and he obeyed.

Pierce sipped and regarded the fugitive. "What happened to your arm?" he eventually asked, in a tone that clearly indicated that Marshal Pierce did not care what had happened to it.

"Broke it," replied the outlaw. "An' it don't help havin' it tied behind my back."

Pierce gestured. "You can untie him, Mister Waite."

The moment Carlin could rub his arms, he did so. "A little whiskey would help," he told Pierce, who handed over the bottle, then took it back after the prisoner had swallowed several times.

Marshal Pierce was comfortable. The violence was over. Dead men were no novelty to him, so he did not take his eyes off the outlaw. "Who shot the freegrazer in Harmonville?"

Carlin bobbed his jaw in the direction of the dark man. "Him."

"What's his name?"

"Brant. Pete Brant. Mister Baxter hired him after I busted my arm."

"How'd you bust it?"

Carlin held out his hand for the bottle, and Pierce handed it to him, then took it back after Carlin had swallowed a couple more times.

"I asked how you busted it."

Carlin shot a sideways look at Charley Waite, standing back there with a Winchester at his side. "Well, I got into a fight with a big cowboy at the store in Harmonville. That's how it got busted, during the tussle."

Marshal Pierce stoppered the bottle and put it aside, lifted out his Colt, and methodically began shucking out empty loads. As he was punching out fresh loads from his shell belt he said, "What was the big cowboy's name?"

"I don't know. Just some big—" Carlin stopped the moment a cold gunbarrel touched the back of his neck.

Pierce raised his eyes, then went back to reloading. "Sure you know his name, Ed."

"It's the gospel truth, marshal. I never heard his name."

"What did you know about him, Ed? Let me tell you something. That feller holdin' the gun to your neck is likely to blow your brains out if you keep on skirtin' answers. What did you know about him?"

"He was a freegrazer. Him and his friends ran cattle over Mister Baxter's range. He told them to move on. Instead, they—" The gun pressure increased.

Charley asked Carlin a question. "If you'd killed the boy that night, nobody would have known who raided the wagon-camp, would they?"

Carlin's face was sweat-shiny. "The boy? What boy?"

Charley cocked the weapon, and Marshal Pierce unwound up off the ground to be well out of the way as he said, "Ed, if you're a prayin' man you'd better start."

Carlin was panting as gun pressure forced his head forward and downward. Charley said it again. "If you'd gone over to make sure the kid was dead, no one ever would have known, would they?"

Carlin gasped. "Marshal, for Chris'sake, you're a lawman, you can't let him—"

Pierce laughed. "With someone like you, Carlin, I'll dance the jig when he pulls the trigger."

Charley slid the gunbarrel over sweaty flesh. Carlin cried out. "Someone said the kid was bleedin' like a stuck hawg. I figured he was dyin'. We had to get the hell away because a couple of them freegrazers was missin'. We ran for it."

Charley said, "How far out were you when you

shot the man in the head who broke your arm? *How far!*"

"Pretty close to where you caught me. Maybe fifteen yards southward."

Marshal Pierce frowned. "That's good shooting for a one-armed man on a dark night."

"Naw. They had a supper fire goin'. We could see 'em real plain."

Charley stepped back, let the Winchester sag, and gazed far out eastward where dawn's weak paleness showed.

Marshal Pierce moved back, nudged the younger man, and said, "Sit up. If you want to blubber, go find a towel. *Sit up!*"

Chapter Twenty-one
A New Day

Marshal Pierce let the little fire die as he emptied the pockets of the prisoners and finished a cigar before arising to stretch. He rubbed his stubbled jaw and looked out where the horses were.

When Charley also stood up, Marshal Pierce looked searchingly at him. "You all right?" he asked.

Charley nodded and started eastward to bring in their horses while the federal officer rolled the dead men in blankets and rounded up ropes to tie them with.

Ed Carlin had watched Charley Waite leave the camp, and with that peculiar camaraderie that professional outlaws shared with professional lawmen, said, "I think that damned fool would have shot me."

Pierce agreed. "I expect he would, and except for the fact that we only got two saddle horses, it wouldn't have bothered me if he did."

"Two horses . . . ?"

Pierce bobbed his head in the direction of the younger rider. "Him and you are going to walk. Mister Waite and I'll ride behind our cantles with these two dead men across the saddle seats."

Carlin protested. "Walk all the way back to Harmonville? I got a splittin' headache. That bastard like to busted my skull."

Marshal Pierce smiled. "You're lucky. Look at your friends. What's that crybaby's name?"

"Joe Evans."

"Get him on his damned feet. And, Carlin, don't give neither of us an excuse on the hike back . . . By the way, in this country they think your name is Butler. Well, I've seen your ivory-handled gun before, so when we get back I'll call you Butler, but as soon as I can get authority to extradite you, you'll be Carlin. You understand?"

Whether the outlaw understood or not, he was given no opportunity to say because Charley had returned with the horses, and for a half hour the two lawmen and the two survivors were occupied in loading and tying the dead men.

The sun was climbing by the time they started across country toward Harmonville. Behind them they left the roundup camp in disarray.

By the time they were out of sight of the camp, with the sun directly overhead, two men riding bareback arrived at the camp. They could interpret what they saw correctly. What they did not know was whether Denton Baxter had been killed or not. They turned northeastward in the direction of the Baxter homeplace. They were the two men sent westward on foot to catch horses.

The heat arrived, shimmering waves of it, before the lawman and the freegrazer reached timber shade. The pair of men walking ahead on foot were wilted, but Dallas Pierce kept them moving by pointing ahead where tall trees stood.

By the time they reached tree shade Carlin was ill, so they had to halt and unburden the horses. Pierce had the whiskey bottle in a saddlebag and handed it to Carlin, but the outlaw waved it away, sank flat out on pine needles, and closed his eyes, his face ashen. The younger rider's face was red and sweat-shiny. He said nothing unless he was spoken to. At this cooler place when Charley offered him whiskey he drank it, and while his mood did not appear to improve at first, he sweated more than ever.

They had no water, so Marshal Pierce went exploring on foot. During his absence, Joe Evans told Charley he had hired on with Baxter three months earlier and until day before yesterday when the crew rode into Harmonville, he'd never before seen a man killed.

Charley listened without expression. When the younger man said, "I was at your wagoncamp," Charley gazed steadily at him. Evans jutted his jaw in the direction of Carlin. "He said we'd just put a hell of a scare into them. After he shot that big feller he told me it was a mistake, that in the dark a man couldn't be real accurate."

Charley asked a question. "And you believed him?"

Evans avoided Charley's gaze while shaking his head. "No. I've seen Ed shoot. He don't miss. Even with that busted arm he don't miss."

Marshal Pierce came back, removed his hat, mopped sweat off, and shook his head. He had found no water.

The outlaw gave no indication that he heard anything that was happening around him. Pierce hoisted him up, propped him against a knee, and got whiskey down him. Carlin's eyes were fixed on the lawman. He blew out a fiery breath and said, "I'll never make it. We ain't even halfway yet. Where's the water?"

Pierce left the outlaw, went over to Charley, and said, "He can ride and I'll walk. Where is the nearest water?"

As far as Charley knew, it was in Harmonville, which is what he told the marshal.

The sun was slanting away when they got under way again, this time with Marshal Pierce leading the horse he had been riding, and with Ed Carlin behind the cantle.

Nothing was said as they trudged through the heat. Joe Evans was suffering and occasionally stumbled. When he did, Marshal Pierce pulled him back to his feet and growled at him.

Charley saw buzzards circling through the blurry heat haze. As he brought his gaze down to the onward land he thought he saw riders, decided it was a mirage, rubbed his eyes, and reset his hat so there would be more shade for his face.

It *was* riders. Seven of them. Marshal Pierce croaked and gestured toward the wavery silhouettes, then halted the horse he had been leading and moved into its shade.

When the horsemen came up and halted, they sat a short moment staring, then swung to the ground with canteens. A moment after Charley drank, sweat burst out all over his body in rivulets.

The leader of the newcomers was, of all people, Judge Ambrose Collins. He was dark with sweat, his face flushed, and when he dismounted he almost fell.

The others were townsmen. Some Charley had seen before, some he had not, but as they trouped back to gaze at the corpses one man stopped to offer Charley the makings, then stood there as Charley rolled a smoke and lighted it. As Charley was handing the makings back, the townsman said, "A bigger posse went south."

Charley trickled smoke. "How'd you fellers happen to come out this way?"

"Just a hunch. Doc Barlow an' a kid stayin' with him thought Baxter would head out here to find his riders. They'd give him an alibi about killing that old freegrazer in town."

Charley stared. "Is he dead?"

"The freegrazer? Yeah, he died real early this morning. Doc Barlow said there wasn't nothing he could do; the old gent had been shot through the guts and was bleedin' internally. But he was tough. He hung on a long while."

Charley dropped the smoke, stepped on it, and went over to his livery horse. The others were ready to ride. Marshal Pierce and Judge Collins had been arguing, but as the cavalcade got under way they rode side-by-side as though there had been no argument.

The men from town were carrying jerky, which they shared with the bedraggled, exhausted, and hollow-eyed men. Two of them rode with Ed Carlin, a man on each side in case he fell. He looked slightly better than he had looked back in the trees, but still had poor color.

Marshal Pierce rode up front with Judge Collins, explaining everything that had happened since he and Charley Waite rode out of Harmonville. The judge was sweating like a stud horse, half listening and half concentrating on what was far ahead, rooftops, shade, beer with peppermint, and something to sit on that wasn't moving. To Ambrose Collins, horses were for pulling things, not to sit on.

It was dusk before the heat diminished, and it was much later and as dark as the inside of a boot when they finally straggled into Harmonville. His Honor left his horse without even looking back and went hobbling painfully in the direction of the saloon.

Marshal Pierce gave the orders. The dead men were placed in a horse stall for the time being. The prisoners were driven up the boardwalk toward the jailhouse, leaving the livery barn nightman to care for all the animals, something he did with a sullen look. Charley stopped at the stone trough out front to put his hat aside, dunk his head several times, then fling off water and start toward the jailhouse with his hat in his hand, letting the night air dry him.

The man behind Marshal Poole's table was Hank Fenwick, who owned the saloon and the poolhall. He stood up as Dallas Pierce pushed his captives into the lighted office, stared in disbelief, and finally got the key ring to lead the way to the cells.

Charley entered the office, where Marshal Pierce was sprawling, but made no move to sit down, and when the saloon owner returned, Charley asked him about Marshal Poole.

The saloonman rehung the key ring and sat down at the table before answering. "During the excitement he left town riding toward the foothills like the devil was behind him. He hasn't come back."

Marshal Pierce gazed at Charley. "He's goin' to be surprised, isn't he? The feller he's riding north to have protect him is lying' down yonder in a horse stall."

The saloonman looked quickly at Pierce. "Baxter?"

"Deader'n a rock, mister. Him and one of his riders named . . . what was his name, Mister Waite?"

"Pete Brant."

"Yes. Pete Brant. He's down there too."

The saloonman looked at Marshal Pierce. "That freegrazer died in the night. Do you know who shot him from down in front of the livery barn?"

Dallas Pierce did not reply, but sat gazing steadily across the room waiting for Charley to supply the answer. He did. "Pete Brant."

The saloonman blew out a long breath and leaned back in his chair. "How'd you two know where they went after the shooting?"

Charley was already moving through the ajar door when Marshal Pierce leaned to shove up to his feet. "By the smell," he said, and left the office a few yards behind Charley.

He caught up with him across the road, walking in the direction of the roominghouse, and strode beside him in silence until they had reached the sagging roominghouse porch, where an almost overwhelming scent of perfume reached the full length of the old building from a massive vine laden with lavender flowers. Dallas Pierce halted, tapped Charley, and said, "In this life, Mister Waite, if it ain't happenin', it's fixin' to. Goodnight. I'm goin' to sleep for a week. Then I'm goin' to eat a cow and set in a tub of water for two hours."

Charley watched the rawboned older man enter the building, then turned to look northward up Main Street as far as the Barlow cottage. It was dark.

He was hungry, but most of all he was too tired even to think straight. Eventually he also entered the roominghouse, where an elderly man with unkempt hair and close-set watery eyes blocked his passage beneath a hanging lamp. "A room is two bits for the night," the man said.

Charley fished for a coin, handed it over, and followed the old man to a room containing a narrow cot, spikes in the wall to hang clothing on, a cigarette-scarred small table holding a white washbasin, and a pitcher of water.

There was a window in the west wall, which Charley had to struggle to open. Immediately that overpowering fragrance swept in, so he half closed the window and went to sit on the edge of the cot and kick out of his boots, remove his hat, and lie back.

Boss had been right: the day of freegrazers was passing. He had also been right about something else; he had been too old for the trouble that went with freegrazing.

He would never buy that saloon and sit comfortably by a crackling stove in wintertime or relax in a cool building during summer.

His cattle were out yonder, mostly rounded up by Baxter's riders, the old campwagon was still in place across the alley from the livery barn, and that son of a bitch who shot Boss had paid for his expert marksmanship.

Charley was drifting off when he thought of

Button. What the hell would become of him now? Whatever it was could wait until morning.

Charley went to sleep. Outside, Harmonville gradually ended this day even up at the saloon, where there had been loud talk for an hour or more after the townsmen returned with a story to tell.

The last sound at the roominghouse came from two grizzled men wearing rider's coats that reached below their knees. They had been drinking at the saloon when those townsmen had returned. Their interest in all the excitement of the roadway shooting following the courtroom hearing was less than everyone else's because they did not know the man who had been shot, nor the town marshal who had fled town. They were just passing through.

They were cattle buyers. As one grumbled to his companion when they entered their room, "We might as well catch the morning coach. This damned place is too upset for a man to do any business."

His friend was closing the door when he replied. "Don't be so damned hasty, Wes. You heard him say this big cowman named Baxter was killed. Well now, think about that."

His friend straightened up from lighting a small lamp. He shucked out of his coat, hung it from a nail, put his hat beside it, and vigorously scratched his head as he faced his partner. "John, I've told you before, you got a real devious mind."

John shed his coat and hat too, but he hung his on the floor. "If I didn't have, Wes, we'd have lost out on a lot of deals. . . . What in hell is that smell?" He walked to the ajar window, sniffed, and slammed the window closed. "Flowers!"

Faintly heard in the room was a wagon being driven southward through town. John cocked his head, wrinkled his brows, and pulled out a large gold watch with elaborate engraving. He flipped open the cover, held the face to the light, and said, "It's after midnight. Who in the hell is driving a rig at this time of night?"

His partner did not reply. He was shedding his boots preparatory to dropping back on his cot.

Chapter Twenty-two
Boss's Note

There was considerable activity in town the following morning, but neither Dallas Pierce nor Charley Waite was part of it.

Harmonville's temporary town marshal, Hugh Fenwick, had repeated what his prisoners at the jailhouse told him when he'd taken food down to them. Some folks were willing to believe it because they had never liked Al Poole, but others were skeptical. If Poole returned, the skeptics would have supported him, but he did not return.

In fact, he never returned.

The riders who had raced southward on the wrong trail had included those three freighters who'd abducted Paul Sawyer and Alf Owens.

They arrived early at the jailhouse, during Hugh Fenwick's interrogation of Ed Carlin and Joe Evans. It was these three men who set Owens and Sawyer against Carlin and Evans, which resulted in the whole story tumbling out—the same story Hugh Fenwick took up to his saloon after leaving the freighters in charge at the jailhouse.

By the time Charley Waite arose to go down to the cafe for breakfast, just about every detail of what had occurred the previous night was common knowledge.

Charley had no idea that he had come out of all the recitations as a hero. There had to be one; every situation of this kind was required to produce one. That was how things were. Dallas Pierce was accorded respect, even some admiration; but lawmen were hired and paid to do what Pierce had done. Besides, he was a federal marshal; there was ambivalence about federal marshals, about lawmen in general.

After breakfast Charley went up to the tonsorial parlor for a shave and haircut. The barber was less inhibited than the diners at the cafe had been. He asked point-blank if it was true that Denton Baxter was dead. Charley replied that it was true. The barber then asked how Baxter had died and who had shot him, and Charley did not say another word, not even after he was presentable and handed over the two bits, which the barber took without a smile.

After leaving the barbershop, Charley went up to the Barlow cottage. Sue and Button were there. When she admitted Charley, Button came from the back of the house to stand in a doorway. Charley tossed aside his hat as he said, "You're looking good."

Button quietly asked if Charley wanted to see Boss, and led the way to a room off the kitchen. The room had only one window and it had been covered by a pale cloth. Boss was lying on the bed as though he were sleeping. In the poor light, Charley could not see the grayness nor the wasted look, but as he stood gazing down he thought Boss looked old, which he had never seemed to be in life.

Button left the room. Sue watched him depart before she spoke. "There was nothing my brother could do. He was bleeding internally. By the time we got him up here he was—"

"Yeah," Charley said quietly, and turned from the bed to look at the handsome woman. "I heard about it yesterday. I guess we could take him out yonder and bury him beside Mose."

Sue was looking at Boss's face when she said, "Walt and I sat with him. I went to Button's room to be with him. He took it very hard."

Charley nodded. "They was close, Sue. Button had no one and neither did Boss. They was good for each other."

"Boss asked for some paper and a pencil. He wrote you a note. It's in my brother's office. I'll get it."

"No. Not right now," Charley said, moving out of the darkened little room.

She followed him to the parlor, where he paused gazing in the direction of Button's room. She waited for him to speak. She had already heard the details of what had happened last night. She knew Baxter was dead and one of his riders, the man who had been identified as the gunman who shot Boss Spearman, was also dead. One of the details she had heard was that the man who shot Boss Spearman had been shot three times at fairly close range; any of the three shots would have resulted in death.

He retrieved his hat and stood holding it in

both hands as he said, "We brought back two prisoners."

She knew that.

"There are two more down at the jailhouse. I guess the federal marshal will take them up to Denver to stand trial."

She raised her brows. "What about Judge Collins?"

He thought about that. "Well, Marshal Pierce said something about extraditing the prisoners. That's between him and the judge, I guess. I don't know much about the law."

"Charley?"

"Yes'm."

"What about Button? What about you?"

"Me? I was lookin' for work when I met Boss. I'll start lookin' again, somewhere."

"And Button?"

He raised his hat to study it. "Boss told me one time he didn't like the notion of Button becomin' a cowman. He wanted him to go to work in a town an' learn a trade."

Sue waited for more, but Charley remained silent for a while, so she said, "He . . . you and Mister Spearman and the big man who was killed, were his family. Charley, we've talked a lot."

"Yes'm."

"Would you like me to tell you what I think?"

"Yes, I would."

"I'm sure he could apprentice out to someone in Harmonville. The harness maker or the blacksmith. Maybe to the gunsmith or the man who owns the abstract office."

Charley nodded and her eyes never left him. "But if you ride on, that will complete his loss. When someone is sixteen years old he can't absorb the shocks of life as well as he can at our age. I think that if you rode on, he would try to find you."

He looked steadily at her. "And if I took him with me, he could most likely get hired on somewhere as a chore boy. Someday he'd become a hired rider. Sue, I don't know anything but cattle and horses, so that's about all I could pass along to him."

She said, "Excuse me for a moment," and disappeared beyond a door on the south side of the parlor next to her brother's examination room. When she returned she was holding a folded paper, which she handed him. "From Mister Spearman."

He nodded, pocketed the paper, and put on his hat as he moved toward the roadway door. She went out onto the porch with him. It was a magnificent day. Instead of the usual rising heat, there was a soft, cool breeze coming in from the east. It loosened a coil of her sorrel hair, which she pushed away with the back of one hand. "Charley, please don't ride on until we've talked again."

He told her he wouldn't do that. He wanted to talk to Button when he was up to it; they'd have to decide where to bury Boss Spearman. Then he left her and walked southward. She watched him. On the opposite side of the road, someone called. Charley stopped and waited for Marshal Pierce to cross over.

The federal officer was clean, shaved, clear-eyed, and evidently fed because he was chewing on a toothpick as he stepped up and nodded at Charley Waite. "The judge got Fenwick to get up a posse and go up to the Baxter place. Collins wants the town marshal brought back, along with anyone else the posse finds up there."

Charley spoke dryly. "All they're goin' to find up there is an empty bunkhouse and maybe some dust. What about the prisoners at the jailhouse?"

"Well, His Honor and I got into an argument about that yesterday. He says they got to be tried here in Harmonville. I want to take them back to Denver to be tried before a federal magistrate. But I got to get an extradition paper from the territorial governor to do that, which might take up to about three weeks."

"So they'll be tried here?"

Pierce shrugged. "I got to wait for the extradition paper anyway, Mister Waite. But His Honor can't do no more than have a hearing."

"Then what happens?"

"Then he'll remand them back to jail with a recommendation that a territorial prosecutor come to Harmonville to try them."

"So you lose out."

"Maybe. But all but that young one, Joe Evans, are fugitives. Poole had posters cached in his office showing them to be wanted by federal authorities."

"So, after they are remanded, you'll get your extradition paper and haul them up to Denver?"

Marshal Pierce smiled. "That's what His Honor an' I been haggling about."

"Marshal, what the hell difference does it make where they're tried?"

Pierce continued to smile. "Ambrose Collins is afraid a federal judge up yonder who wasn't down here an' who won't know everything will maybe sentence them to a few years in prison. He wants to turn his hearing into a formal trial for the feller you know as Ed Butler, and sentence him to hang for murder. He don't want the others to get off any lighter than the maximum the law says."

Charley flapped his arms. None of this was more than passingly interesting to him. As far as he was concerned the whole damned dirty mess was finished. His personal urge to settle up for Boss had been satisfied. "Just tell me one thing," he said to the lawman. "Will Butler, or whatever his name is, get off easy if he's tried in Denver?"

"If you mean will he hang, I'll guess that he will. A man can't ever be sure what a judge will do, but like I told Judge Collins, in my experience they're just as hard on killers in Denver as he'd be down here. An' they got more authority."

Charley saw Doctor Barlow across the road in front of the general store, so he said, "Good luck," and walked on an angling course to the far plank-walk.

Walt Barlow had been down at the apothecary's shop. He greeted Charley with a "Good morning," then asked if Charley had been up at his cottage. Charley nodded. "Yes. As soon as I can hitch up our campwagon I'll take Boss back out where we were livin' and bury him."

"What about Button? Will you take him along?"

"I don't like the idea, doctor, but he'd sure never forget it if I didn't."

Barlow watched a fringed-top buggy pass northward as he said, "My sister could go along, Mister Waite."

Charley stared. "Why?"

Barlow's gaze returned from the buggy to Charley's face. "Because Sue and Button have become very close. It'll be hard on him out there. He's somewhere between boyhood and manhood."

"She might not want to go, doctor."

Barlow's reply indicated he and his sister had already discussed this. "She'll go. She's fond of Button. Women like my sister have a powerful mothering instinct. Would you object to her going?"

Charley had to think this over. He'd had no inkling that this might come up. He turned at the sound of loud voices over in front of the jailhouse, where Judge Collins and Marshal Pierce were arguing as they pushed open the jail-house door and went inside.

He turned back. "No objection."

After Doctor Barlow departed, walking briskly northward, Charley entered the saloon, which had a few midday customers, and a barman he had never seen before. He took a bottle with a jolt glass to a far table, shoved back his hat, filled the little glass, fished out the paper Sue Barlow had given him, and after downing the whiskey, unfolded it, certain it would be Boss's farewell to him, perhaps with some of Boss's homespun wisdom and a few admonitions.

He was wrong. There was no philosophy and no admonitions. Boss had evidently known he did not have time for those things. The note, signed by Boss and witnessed by Sue Barlow, was short and to the point. It was Boss's last testament. It bequeathed everything Boss owned to Charley—his cattle, the old wagon, his personal effects, and his last prayer that, as his sole heir, Charley would look after Button.

Charley reread the note, placed it on the table, and refilled the jolt glass. He downed its contents, pushed both glass and bottle away, and read the note again.

When the barman came to see if he wanted anything else, Charley shook his head, handed over some silver, and told the barman to take the whiskey away. Then he leaned back in the chair, shoved his feet out beneath the table, and gazed at the farthest wall.

So much for saddling up and riding on.

He was still sitting there a half hour later when two raffish older men came in to lean on the bar. They wore almost identical long rider's coats. He heard one of them ask the barkeeper for directions to the Baxter ranch. They were interested in buying cattle, and since they had heard Baxter was dead, they wondered if the barman could tell them who his heir might be before they made that long a ride.

The barman answered with the authority of a man whose knowledge had been gathered over a number of years of listening to saloon talk. In a place like Harmonville, in any cowtown for that matter, the best source of local information, gossip, and slander, was the most frequented bar.

"Mister Baxter has a sister living back in Chicago. She visited him at the ranch three years ago. His foreman, a feller named Vince Ballester, told me one time she was Mister Baxter's only kin."

The cattle buyers exchanged a long-faced look. One of them said, "Chicago? Who'd know her address back there?"

The barman did not know. "Ballester might have, but he got a broken hip a while back in some kind of brawl out on the range, and the last I heard he'd went down to Albuquerque to see a doctor. You gents might ride up there; there should be someone around who could help."

Charley watched the cattle buyers lean their heads together after the barman walked away. They conversed like conspirators for several minutes, then left the saloon.

Chapter Twenty-three
The Last Drive Out

The weather was beautiful. Visibility to the north was limited only by the mountains, and to the west by the soft blending of earth and sky. Wild grass, revitalized by the storm, rose tall enough to rub wheelhubs as the old camp-wagon passed the place where Charley and Marshal Pierce had met the riders from town with their canteens.

Sue Barlow held Button's hand while Charley drove in the shade of the rain-tightened canvas over the bows. In back, Boss Spearman had been propped on both sides with bedrolls.

They were within sight of the old camp by nightfall, and they continued through the darkness until they reached it. After caring for the team, Charley dropped the tailgate, set the poles for the texas, then took digging tools and walked southward, leaving Button and Sue to make camp.

A half hour later with a yellow moon rising, Button came out with another shovel. Charley climbed out and handed Button down. Charley drank from a canteen, rolled and lit a smoke, and gazed back where the texas reflected the supper fire. He could see Sue working at the fire.

Button tired quickly, so Charley pulled him out and climbed back down. From up above Button said, "There's no sign of the cattle."

His answer came from below the ground. "They're a mile or so beyond the creek where Baxter's crew camped while they rounded them up. They won't have drifted much. Not with feed to their hocks."

"They rounded them up?"

"Yeah, Button. Seems Baxter'd done this before. Run off freegrazers, scatter their cattle, then catch 'em after the freegrazers was scairt out of the country and drive 'em up north an' sell 'em."

"Charley?"

"Yeah?"

"Did you find out who shot Boss?"

"Yeah."

"Who was he, one of Baxter's riders?"

"Yeah. Feller named Pete Brant."

"Is he the other one Doctor Barlow brought up from the livery barn to embalm before they bury them?"

"Yeah."

"Charley . . . ?"

The voice from below ground level spoke quietly. "Button, it's finished with. Talking about it won't change anything. You were going to ask me who shot that feller who shot Boss. It don't matter. He's dead. . . . Hand me down the canteen, will you?"

There was no more conversation until the grave

was ready and Charley climbed up to lean on the shovel, wrinkling his nose as the fragrance of cooking food came down to him.

As they were walking back he slapped Button roughly on the shoulder. "You're still a little puny."

"I'll be all right in a week or so. Miss Barlow said so."

Charley repositioned the shovel he was carrying so that it would not gouge his shoulder. "Did you ever know a lady like her?"

"No. I think my mother must have been like her."

"You don't remember your mother?"

"She died when I was born. My paw . . . he stayed around until she was buried, then I never saw him again. . . . Charley?"

"What?"

"After we bury Boss, what will we do?"

Charley shifted the shovel again and looked ahead where Sue was bending over the fire. He had no idea their voices carried to her through the still night. "We gather all the cattle. Boss left half to you and half to me. I think we ought to sell them, but you got an interest so what we do with them'll be your decision too."

Button looked shocked as he watched Charley's profile. Finally he said, "All of them?"

"Yeah. And the horses, the wagon, his weapons, and his gatherings. Half to you, half to me. Think on it tonight, Button. Take your time. The cattle won't drift much and they'll be packin' more lard under their hides on the new grass."

Sue had coffee and a full meal for them. Charley was impressed by her efficiency at camping. He told her the grave was completed and that they'd bury Boss about sunup, which had been Boss's favorite time of day.

Button went after his bedroll and carried it up front, where the wagon tongue was lying in the grass. Sue refilled Charley's coffee cup, watched him roll and light a smoke, and said, "Did you read Mister Spearman's note?"

He nodded while lighting the quirley.

She looked steadily at him. "So did I when I witnessed it."

He pitched the firebrand back into the fire and glanced up because he felt her eyes on him. He smiled at her. "Well, that's the way he would have left things if he'd been up to it."

She smiled back. "You knew him better than I did. All I know is that he didn't divide things like that."

He sipped black coffee, put the cup down, and blew smoke at the vault of heaven. "There'd be no point in telling Button."

She agreed. "No point at all. Charley . . . you're a really fine man."

He sat like a stone, looking into the fire for a long time, too startled at first even to look at her. As he stared into the fire, he grew downright uncomfortable.

Eventually he said, "If you want, I'll put your bedroll here by the fire before I turn in."

She declined the offer. "I can do it."

He stood up, still avoiding her face. "Goodnight. That was about as good a supper as I've ever had."

"Goodnight, Charley."

He bedded down up front, a few yards from Button, which gave Sue the privacy of the rear of the wagon. He rested his head on his hands and watched the stars until he was drowsy. Button's quiet voice said, "I guess we'd ought to do like you said and sell the cattle. We don't own any land, an' like Boss said, freegrazing seems to be about finished. Ever since we been moving there's been some kind of trouble. Even in the towns we passed through, folks didn't like us. Only, what'll we do without the cattle?"

Charley yawned before answering. "Darned if I know. I've been looking at the back end of cattle since I was about your age. I never thought about living different, partner." He yawned again. "You got any ideas?"

"No. Except that living in town . . . I don't know, Charley."

The older man listened to Button's voice trailing off, and intuitively felt the youth's indecision.

He felt his way by saying, "It's got its advantages, Button," and waited to see what the response would be.

"Yeah, I reckon it does. The roofs don't leak like a wagon canvas and . . ."

"And what?"

Button was squirming. "Those freighters," he said.

Charley's intuition brought him wide awake. Button wasn't thinking about the freighters; not the male ones anyway. "That girl's nice," Charley said.

Button's reply seemed to have been dragged out of him. "Annie? Yeah, she's nice. Only she's awful young."

"What'd she be, you reckon; about twelve?"

"Something like that. An' that's awful young."

Charley smiled in the darkness. "They grow up fast, Button. You're only maybe four years older than she is. In another couple of years you'll be eighteen and she'll be about fourteen, or thereabouts. I saw some other girls down there."

"Yeah . . . there were some."

Charley smiled up at the winking stars. "We better get some sleep, partner. See you in the morning."

Ten minutes later Button was snoring and Charley, who had been fighting sleep at the beginning of their talk, was now wide awake.

In the morning he did not remember falling to sleep. Sue was already at her cooking fire when Charley rolled out. It was a long walk to the willow creek to wash. When he got there the smell of cattle was strong, although they had left their beds earlier and were no longer visible by predawn light.

On the way back he met Button hiking along with a towel over his shoulder and a chunk of tan lye soap in one hand. They exchanged smiles, spoke briefly, and continued on their way, Button toward the creek, Charley toward the camp, where Sue had breakfast waiting.

He sat on the ground watching her work. She threw him a smile. "Did you sleep well?" she asked, and when he replied that he'd slept like a log she said, "But not for an hour or so." He stared at her, getting redder by the minute, but she said no more and turned back to the fire. *She had heard everything he and Button talked about!*

She handed him a cup of coffee, eyes twinkling. "You shouldn't be surprised, Charley."

He tried the coffee; it was as hot as the hubs of hell.

"He's sixteen years old," she said.

He held the cup by the handle to avoid burning his fingers.

"You continually surprise me," she said. "Have you ever been married?"

"No, ma'am."

"Then you must have had brothers or sisters."

"No. No family at all."

She studied him for a moment. "Then how did you know the right things to tell him last night?"

He tried the coffee and had to lower the cup again. She was waiting for him to speak so he said, "I don't know as I told him the right things. I just figured what was on his mind. Sue, we been together for a while. You get to know folks best when you're on the move an' in camp with them." He jutted his jaw in the direction of the golden-brown fried potatoes and the crisp meat. "Where did you learn to cook over an open fire? You're better'n any man I ever knew who did it."

She accepted the compliment as his way of changing the subject. When Button came along she fed them both and was mostly quiet. She was thinking now about the part they had to do next.

They hitched the wagon to its team and drove out to the graveside. Button and Charley got Boss out, wrapped him completely, and used ropes to lower his body. Sue watched from the shade of the wagon. She moved only when they went for the shovels to begin the filling.

She said a long prayer, which stopped both the shovelers. When she had finished and returned to the wagon, they shoveled the grave full, moving easily, almost effortlessly as men do when engaged in manual labor while their minds are elsewhere.

When it was done Sue returned and stood with them beside the mounded grave, looking at the crest of higher earth that would eventually settle to ground level. By next year, grass would almost completely conceal the fact that this was a grave.

She said another long prayer. Charley watched her. She had never mentioned religion, but he could not believe she hadn't memorized those prayers long ago. She had a soft, clear voice.

The sun was climbing when they struck camp and headed back toward Harmonville. As before, when they were sitting together on the wagon seat, nothing was said for a long time.

Charley did not believe they could reach town before dark, and was going over in his mind the places he had seen along this route where they could camp. What he had never seen between the distant creek behind them and Harmonville was water. Neither springs nor creeks.

They had a short keg of water in the wagon, so they could get through the night, but the team would do better if there was flowing water.

Sue broke the silence by pointing toward a spit of trees. "There is a sump spring back in there. I know it's a little early to set up camp, but between that spring and town there is no other water."

Charley swung the wagon toward the trees. When it was lined out he looked at her. She read his mind. "I ride over the countryside whenever I can. I love open land. Since we've been here, there is very little of the range I don't know."

Button looked steadily at her. "Do you own a horse?" he asked. She smiled and wagged her head. "No. I take a livery animal. But someday I'm going to own a horse. I'm very fond of horses."

Button sat watching the trees come down to them. Charley drove in silence as far as the first overripe pines and firs, then stood up to look for passage into the timber. He guided the horses until they were in deep, fragrant shade with a small, horseshoe-shaped clearing on their right.

They all climbed down to set up camp. While Button was helping Charley hobble the team out in the little meadow he said, "Maybe when we go back to gather the cattle we could look for our loose stock."

Charley nodded.

"And we could give her one of them."

Charley arose stiffly to watch one of the horses hop out to graze. "Good idea," he said. They stood together for a while watching the hitch, then started back where Sue had a cooking fire glowing, its light gray smoke rising straight up in the windless sky.

This time all three of them helped with the meal, but Sue gave the orders. She waited until they had been fed, then led off across the little meadow past the horses to the far side of it, where there was a fairly well-marked game trail. She went unerringly to a marshy place alive with gnats.

The sump spring had water in its center. To get out there to drink, one would have to wade through mud.

She worried about the large harness horses getting bogged in mud with their hobbles. Charley reassured her. "They can handle something like that without trouble."

On the way back to camp Button veered off for his own reason and disappeared up through the timber. Sue had covered another twenty yards before she said, "When Mister Spearman was dying he told me how he'd found Button. He also told me his real name: John Weatheral. Charley, isn't sixteen a little old to be still calling him Button?"

He thought it probably was, but as he told her, they'd all been calling the kid Button for so long that it might take a while before he'd know they were talking to him if they started calling him John.

They crossed the little clearing and paused at the outer limits of the camp. She brushed his arm with her hand. "Wouldn't it be uncomplicated if this was what life was all about?"

He looked at her. "You're a town woman, Sue."

She laughed and strode forward. "Not at heart. In springtime and autumn I dream of driving out here somewhere in an old wagon and making a camp."

He followed her into camp without taking his eyes off her.

Chapter Twenty-four
A Seal-brown Horse

They reached Harmonville a little past noon the following day after an early start. Sue left them down at the public corrals to hasten home. Her brother was returning to the kitchen from the embalming shed across the alley and greeted her with a big smile. He went to the stirrup pump to fill a basin as he said, "How'd Button hold up?"

"Fine. Better than I expected," she said, and shook the blueware coffeepot. It was empty so she scrubbed it as they talked and made a fresh potful.

"If the circumstances had been different, Walt, the drive out, the camping, the cooking over an open fire, and driving back would have been perfect."

She watched him dry his hands and go to the table to await the coffee. "And you?"

"I embalmed Baxter and his cowboy. They'll be

buried this afternoon. Marshal Pierce and Judge Collins got into an argument night before last at the saloon. This morning when I went down to the cafe for breakfast, they were sitting together and talking like there'd never been an argument."

"What was the argument about?"

"The judge was mad because he'd expected to spend one day in Harmonville and he's spent close to a week and still hasn't been able to hold a decent court. He was yelling that this sort of thing set him back a week on his schedule so's he wouldn't be anywhere that he was supposed to be for the rest of the season, and folks in all those towns would raise hell with him."

Sue brought two cups to the table and sat down. "But he's going to hold court?"

"No," her brother said with a twinkle. "That's what caused the eruption. Marshal Pierce went down to Kelseyville and sent a telegraph to Santa Fe and got back a telegraphed approval for extradition, then rode back to Harmonville in time for a drink before bedtime, and ran into the judge at the saloon and showed him the telegraph message."

"Wasn't there one of those prisoners who wasn't a fugitive, Walt?"

He shrugged. "I think I heard something about that. . . . This is good coffee."

She smiled. "It tastes that way every once in a while after the pot is scoured and the grounds are fresh."

He left to visit a patient. She was three days behind on her household chores. She worked methodically, doing chores she could have done with her eyes closed, and thought of Button and Charley. When someone rolled bony knuckles over the roadway door she went swiftly to the front of the house and was smiling when she opened the door. The smile faded.

A beard-stubbled man with perpetually narrowed eyes and skin the color of old copper removed his hat and introduced himself with a flourish that made his hat brush against his long rider's coat. "Ma'am, my name is John Welton. This here is my business associate, Wes Long. He was told over at the saloon you might know where he could find a gent named Charley Waite."

She was trying to place them; she was sure she'd seen them before. "He might be at the jailhouse, or the roominghouse."

"No ma'am, we already been to those places. And the saloon."

She had a hunch. "Did you try the livery barn?"

They hadn't. "No ma'am, but we'll go down there." John Welton fidgeted as his partner stood like stone, gazing at the handsome woman. Welton said, "It's about some cattle we heard he's got somewhere out yonder. We're livestock buyers."

She remembered now where she had seen them: standing together in front of the cafe. "If I see him I'll tell him you are looking for him."

Welton smiled. "We're obliged," he said and walked halfway to the front gate before putting his hat on. He said something to his companion as they turned southward toward the lower end of town.

Sue went back to work.

A large freight outfit drawn by six pairs of Mexican mules came into town from the north with the driver and swamper on the high seat. Other roadway traffic had to yield. Behind the wagon a dozen or so yards, far enough back to avoid dust, a solitary horseman rode along looking left and right, an obvious stranger to Harmonville.

The freight wagon turned down the eastside alley to the dock behind the general store. The mounted stranger continued southward to the livery barn. He was not a tall man, nor was he particularly thick, but he had a look of confidence in himself. He asked the hostler where a man named Hugh Fenwick could be found and was directed to the jailhouse or the saloon.

As he was removing his gloves, folding them under his shell belt, Charley Waite came up out of the barn trailed by Button. They had been back at the wagon.

The stranger turned, watched Charley come up out of the barn gloom, and said, "I'll be damned."

Charley grinned. "Yes, you will. It's been a long time, Frank."

The stranger shoved out a hand. "You're lookin' good, Charley. Still freegrazin'?"

Waite gripped the hand and released it. He introduced Button. The stranger extended his hand while eyeing the tall youth. "You know you're in bad company, son?"

Charley and the stranger laughed. Button smiled a little uncertainly until Charley said, "Frank Cole and I rode together years back. We put in some rough times together. Frank, you're passin' through?"

"No. I got a letter from a man named Fenwick. Charley, about the time you hired on with that freegrazer I went to workin' for the law. This feller Fenwick wrote me up at Raton so I came down to see what he's got to offer. He said they needed a town marshal down here."

Charley gazed out into the roadway. Two raffish older men were approaching, wearing almost identical rider's coats that reached below their knees. He had seen them before. As he swung his attention back to Frank Cole he said the same thing the hostler had told the stranger. "Try the jailhouse or the saloon. He owns the saloon and the poolhall. He's been acting town marshal since the former one pulled out in a hurry."

Cole nodded slowly. "Trouble?"

"Fenwick will tell you. Frank, look me up this evening. We'll talk."

Cole nodded, winked at Button, and passed the approaching cattle buyers on his way to the jailhouse.

Charley was turning away when one of the cattle buyers hailed him. "Mister Waite?"

Charley turned back, nodding.

"Well, Mister Waite, this here is my partner Wes Long, an' I'm John Welton. We're livestock buyers. The lady up at the doctor's place told us we might find you down here."

The two men stopped, nodded to Button, and waited. Charley looked them over. He'd met livestock buyers many times. These two looked typical. He did not ask how they knew he might have cattle to sell, but simply said, "It's a big herd, gents."

Wes Long seemed pleased. "Fine. We'd like to ride out an' look 'em over if you don't mind. We got the latest market reports from Omaha. If they're in good flesh we'd like to buy 'em."

Charley looked at Button. "This here is my partner, John Weatheral. He'll ride out there with you. It's a mite late in the day and it's a long ride."

Wes Long rubbed his hands together. "First

thing in the morning then." He turned toward Button. "We could meet you down here. We got to hire horses. Maybe about six o'clock, Mister Weatheral?"

Button said nothing, only nodded his head. After the livestock buyers had departed he turned a worried expression toward Charley. "I don't know anything about selling cattle. You should go out there with them."

Charley was watching the two buyers cross the road up by the saloon, long coats flapping, when he replied, "Just show 'em the cattle. Tell 'em to make their offer and that we'll decide whether to sell or not when you get back." He smiled at the gangling youth. "Mister Weatheral, while you're out yonder I'll see what I can turn up about the Omaha market. If their offer matches it, we'll talk it over when you get back."

Button's anxious expression did not leave. "But . . ."

"Partner, you're not going to learn any younger." He slapped Button on the back and struck out in the direction of the cafe with Button trudging worriedly at his side. Just before they went inside Charley halted and said, "Button, you're growin' up. It's time you tried out bein' a man."

"Charley, I never done anything like this before. There was always you and—"

"You're not goin' to sell the herd, partner, just ride out there, show them the cattle, an' let them make their offer. Button, you got to start sometime. Now let's get something to eat."

"They know I'm just a kid."

Charley was reaching for the door when he replied. "The one who talked called you Mister

Weatheral. Folks don't call kids mister. Quit worrying."

But that was easier said than done. An hour later when they were back down at the wagon, Button said, "Charley, I'm worried."

The older man was fumbling with horse harness draped over the wagon tongue when he replied, "Button, you're a man. You've seen a man killed, you've buried two men, you darn near got killed yourself. You been through one of the worst storms I've ever seen. You've drove cattle with men, you've lived in wagoncamps with them, doing a man's work." Charley stopped straightening the harness and turned. "An' you got the stirrings all men get about your age. Boyhood is behind you, partner."

Charley fished in a trouser pocket, brought forth some silver, and handed it to Button. "Go down to the roominghouse and get yourself a room. I got one down there. I'll be along later. If I miss seein' you when you ride out in the morning, I'll be waitin' when you get back."

He left the youth standing beside the old wagon and struck out up the alley northward. Button watched him go with trepidation and a slowly awakening resolve.

Charley crossed through a weedy place between buildings, emerged on Main Street, and slackened off as he approached the gate out front of the Barlow cottage.

Sue came from the back of the house, opened the door, and smiled. "Some cattle buyers were looking for you," she said as she stepped aside for him to enter.

"I met them. Button's goin' out with them in the morning to show them the cattle."

She did not raise her eyebrows nor say what he expected: that Button was a boy. She led the way to the kitchen, where she'd been preparing supper for her brother, who was out on a call, and invited Charley to share the meal. He declined and sat down, dropping his hat beside the chair.

She went back to the stove. It was hot in the kitchen, and fragrant. He watched her for a moment before saying, "Was everything all right when you got back?"

She replied without turning. "Yes. Did you know they buried Mister Baxter and his cowboy today?"

"No."

"And that Marshal Pierce got authorization from Santa Fe to extradite his prisoners to Denver?"

He hadn't known that either. "What about the judge?"

She turned. I heard he was upset, but I don't think he really objected too much. He's been complaining for days that he's been delayed here in Harmonville. . . . Charley?"

"Yes'm?"

"Those cattle buyers looked like a pair of schemers to me."

He nodded. "That goes with cattle buying. Don't worry. They'll make an offer. When Button gets back we'll talk it over. If their offer is too low, the cattle will stay out there putting on tallow and we'll find another buyer. I'll get a newspaper down at the general store in the morning and see what the Omaha market is paying."

Her brother arrived a few minutes later. He poured two stiff jolts, one for himself, one for Charley Waite, and dropped wearily down at the table. "I've had to take chickens, garden vegetables, homemade white lightning, even some pigs a time or two instead of money. Today I had a choice between probably never getting paid for delivering a baby, or accepting a horse. It's a handsome seal-brown gelding." He dropped the whiskey straight down, blew out a noisy breath, and looked at Charley as his sister piled two plates with food and put them on the table. "Charley, do you want to buy a good horse?"

Charley answered after a moment. "If he's sound and don't have a lot of bad habits, I'll buy him. How much?"

"I charge four dollars for delivering babies."

Charley frowned. "Any horse that's standin' up is worth more than four dollars, Walt. Do you know this horse?"

"Yes. Sue, where's Charley's supper?"

Before she answered, Charley explained that he and Button had eaten at the cafe. Then he repeated, "Do you know this horse?"

Doctor Barlow was pulling his chair closer to the table when he answered. "Yes. I've seen them ride and drive him. He's strong and quiet, doesn't bite or kick or buck, and I mouthed him; he's seven years old."

"Fifteen dollars, but I got to put some sweaty saddleblankets under him to try him first."

Walt had his fork poised. "Fifteen dollars? All right. I took him down to board at the livery barn. Help yourself." He started eating. After a while he said, "I thought you had some horses."

"Yeah, we do have, somewhere out with the cattle."

"Why do you need another one?"

Charley was leaning to retrieve his hat from the

floor when he replied. "For your sister."

Doctor Barlow did not stop chewing, nor even looked up. His reason was elemental: he had wondered if Charley Waite and his sister hadn't been growing fond of each other, and since her return from the wagon trip he had noticed a slight change in her. She smiled more, laughed easily, and lighted up like a Christmas tree when she was talking about Waite and Button. Walt Barlow was not just a good general practitioner, but an experienced diagnostician. He could analyze all kinds of symptoms: not always symptoms of illness.

Chapter Twenty-five
Two Cigars

They left Walt to finish supper alone. Sue hadn't really done much more than pick at her food, so when Charley was ready to leave and she said she'd see him out, her brother nodded and concentrated on his meal. He had been ravenous before the drink of whiskey, and it had only increased his hunger.

Outside, the day had ended and the evening was warm. There were stars in every direction, without any clouds. The moon was still a little lopsided, but it was pewter-bright.

Charley paused on the porch looking southward, down where a few lights showed the length of Main Street. He quietly spoke his thoughts. "It's a nice town, Sue."

She agreed. "I think it is. Charley, it occurred to me that people need something like that storm to rid themselves of inhibitions. You're not a free-grazer to them anymore."

He breathed deeply of the pure, faintly fragrant night air. She waited for him to speak. When he didn't, she asked a question that had been in her mind for several days. "What will you do, you and Button?"

He turned toward her. "I don't know. But once we're shed of the cattle we'll have time to figure it out."

"Ranching, Charley?"

He ruefully smiled. "No, I've been handling cattle most of my life. I got to agree with something Boss said. Button shouldn't grow up knowing nothing but livestock."

"How about you?"

"When the cattle are sold I won't have to worry about livestock anymore. Sue?"

"Yes?"

"There's a harness shop in town."

"Yes. Old Mister Garnet owns it."

"Maybe he'd sell out."

She smiled at him, softly. "Maybe. Walt's been taking care of him for years. It's not just his eyes; he has chest trouble every winter."

He continued to gaze at her. "If you got any suggestions, I'd sure like to hear them."

She didn't have, but she had something else, so she said, "Just don't leave."

He moved to the porch railing to lean there. "No, we'll stay. Sue, if I was to ask you a question . . . ?"

"I'd answer it."

"You never got married?"

It was not the question she expected. "No. I

almost did once, back in Missouri. He died. That was a long time ago. Do you know how old I am, Charley?"

He'd never been able to guess ages in people. He could tell a horse by his teeth, but he'd heard that didn't work with people. "I don't care how old you are."

"I'm not a girl, Charley."

He grinned. "You sure fooled me. I thought you were. Maybe eighteen or nineteen."

"Twenty-five. I'll be twenty-six in three months. That's an old maid."

He still smiled. "Naw. If you're an old maid, why then I got to be decrepit. Thirty-five." He stopped smiling. "What's age got to do with it?"

She moved from overhang shadows to moonlight. To Charley she looked eighteen, and beautiful. "I worry about you two, Charley. You and Button."

"Well now, we worry about you."

"Why?"

He'd had no trouble with words up to now. "Well, for one thing you didn't own a horse."

Her eyes widened.

"For another thing . . . you're a mighty fine cook."

"Anything else?"

"Yeah," he replied, turning his head to look northward beyond town, where the distant mountains looked like smoke.

"Charley . . . ?"

"I'm thinking, Sue," he said, still without looking at her. He let his breath out. "I busted a tooth one time back in Texas. A doctor had to whittle out the stump." He abruptly swung back to face her, the hint of a grin on his face. "An' I thought that was bad, but compared to this, it wasn't bad at all."

"Compared to what?"

"Well . . . tellin' you somethin' you might not want to hear, and ruinin' a friendship."

"Tell me anyway."

"You won't get mad?"

She sighed to herself. He was nice-looking, and considerate and generous. He was kindly. He was also as thick as an oak! "No, I promise not to get mad."

"I'm in love with you. I been that way since you took care of Button. You're the handsomest woman I ever saw. But you got a lot more than that." He stopped.

She moved close to him at the porch railing. "Thank you," she murmured. "Now can I tell you something?" She didn't await an answer, because she knew he did not arrive at decisions quickly. "It was wonderful out there in that camp near the sump spring. I'll remember that as one of the most beautiful experiences of my life. . . . Charley?"

"Yes'm?"

"Will you marry me?"

His jaw sagged. He stared. Finally he smiled. "That's what I been building up to say."

"I hoped you might be, but I've never been very good at waiting. Will you?"

"Yes, ma'am. First thing in the morning. Before breakfast. In fact, right now tonight if there's a person in Harmonville."

She leaned and kissed him gently. "There is a Methodist preacher in Harmonville. Could Button stand up with you? You're supposed to have a best man."

He laughed, thinking that when Button got back he would be faced with another step on his climb toward manhood. "I'd like that. Only he won't be back for about three days."

She already knew that; she'd been out there and back. "We can tell my brother. Tomorrow we can go see the preacher."

He opened his arms, and she came up against him full length, her arms raised to his shoulders.

Her brother opened the door and stood framed in the lamplight. He stood there like a tree for a moment, then stepped back and soundlessly closed the door. He looked at the parlor floor briefly, then went to his office for a cigar. For *two* cigars, he thought, before he started back to the front door.